The Gift

The Gift

stories by

Wayne Connolly

Pontburn Press

ISBN: 978-1-3999-4067-2

Cover illustration and design: Stevie Mitchell
                                         www.inkyconditions.co.uk

Typesetting: Mike Farren

Printed by: ImprintDigital.com

Contents

*For all the good people working
in the Northern Centre for Cancer Care
at the Freeman Hospital, Newcastle upon Tyne.*

And for Angela, wherever she may be.

The Gift

One

Here's a guilty secret. When I was told I had cancer it made me more interesting than I was before. If not to others, at least to myself. It didn't make me brave, or tragic, or more worthy of sympathy, but it gave my shapeless life a new definition. It gave me a story to tell.

I don't know when and where it will end – almost certainly in relapse, possibly in fear and pain. But that's for the future. Now I am looking back for a point of origin, a single moment in time when interesting things began to happen to me...

On my drive home from work I was held up in traffic every day at the same place, near a roundabout at Cowgate, next to Morrisons. The layout of the area had recently changed, the road had been resurfaced and the pavement edged with artificial grass. Each time I stopped, I looked with a new intensity. I was fascinated by the surfaces I saw around me. There was a strange joy in them. Isn't it amazing that we can make these things, I thought. That we can cover the earth with them. I learned what it meant to caress something with your eyes, with a closeness that is almost tactile. And the longer I stared, the more abstracted I felt, as though the world was flattening into planes and angles, and that if I stayed there long enough I would disappear. I think I realise now that I wanted to disappear, for the limits of my body to be erased.

Two

I must have been very young when I first became aware of someone who had cancer. It wasn't called cancer then, of course, at least not in my hearing. Even years later my mother would only whisper it under her breath, as though it was something shameful. Why was the word so hidden? Was it embarrassment or fear? Or something darker, like disgust?

Auntie Winnie lived in Valletort Place, at the bottom of my gran's road near the creek. I didn't see her very often and she almost certainly wasn't an aunt. Possibly a great aunt, or other distant relative. Every older woman was called auntie in those days. She always wore a long coat – that much I remember – and her hair was very red. She might have lived alone, but I can't even be sure of that.

I heard my grandmother and auntie Edna talking quietly to my mother in the kitchen:

She never told anyone, you know.

Nobody would have known if it wasn't for the smell.

If you went to her house the smell was so bad, like something rotten. And it was coming from her.

She took off her blouse and there it was, a hole in her chest, all open and rotten.

And I wonder why Winnie didn't tell anyone. Was that also fear and shame? Or just the quiet need not to make a fuss? The same as my mother when she fell and broke her pelvis fifty years later, and didn't say a word.

Three

Men's illnesses were always more public. They were put on view for family and visitors to share. My grandfather's bed was brought into the front room and everyone sat around, talking about him rather than to him.

How's he getting on?

Has the doctor been?

Have you seen the state of his leg?

The word I remember was gangrene, and it sounded like a colour. I heard more whispered conversations as I stood in the doorway.

It's a disgrace. He shouldn't be left like that.

It's gone black up to his knee.

One day I was watching TV while he lay in bed in the corner of the room. Gran, mum and the others were in the kitchen. He called out, spoke to me, asked for something – it was hard to tell. And all I felt was fear. I had become afraid of my grandad because he was ill, and I ran to get away from him.

As I was growing up, illness was something that happened to old people. It made them frightening and grotesque, so you couldn't bear to look at them. It rotted their bodies and emptied their minds.

Four

The first time I collapsed was into wet grass on a sunny morning.

It had seemed like a good idea to drive from Oslo to Røros overnight in a borrowed car. In midsummer it would never get dark, so the route was easy to follow and the roads quiet all the way. But it had been a hot day, full of busy preparation for the journey, so we were tired even before we set out. Then after three hours the car broke down at a filling station and petrol poured through its damaged fuel tank onto the forecourt. We stood around for two hours waiting for a pickup truck and a replacement car. It was strange to feel so tired with the sky full of light.

We arrived in Røros at seven in the morning and found the wooden cabin in the middle of a field. The day was already bright and the sky clear and blue. I opened the door of the car and fell out sideways. Every pulse of energy that had sustained me through the night seeped away onto the long grass. I lay on my back, completely still, as the cold dew soaked through my clothes and into my hair. And I wanted nothing more than to sink into the deep earth and sleep there for a long time.

I fell again in another country – in Latvia on a weekend trip to Riga. After a full day of walking we were looking for a restaurant on the edge of the city, but we never found it. There were too many dark corners and streets without names. When we headed back to the centre, trying to find somewhere else to eat, I stumbled into a doorway. It wasn't unexpected this time. I knew it would happen. The effort of walking, of carrying on at all, seemed impossible. There was nothing I could do but give in to the need to fall.

Later I told a doctor about this collapse, and she said that I must have run out of fuel. I thought that I had run out of courage. Now I know that my blood was running out on me.

Five

My grandfather had his leg amputated, then he died in hospital of pneumonia. I must have been told these things because I remember them now, but at the time I just knew he wasn't there anymore.

On the day of his funeral, relatives arrived from South Wales and I watched them get out of cars, shaking hands and hugging each other. The women sniffed into tissues and drank sherry from small glasses in gran's flat. I was probably wearing my school uniform, walking from room to room trying not to be noticed. As I passed her, auntie Edna caught hold of me, pulled me close and said, 'You can cry if you want to'. And I thought, why would I do that? Why would I want to cry?

Uncle John died as well, a year later. He was my father's eldest brother. When I went to school I told everyone that his brain had burst. I had seen a brain on TV, in a sci-fi programme. It was a giant brain that filled a whole room, pulsing with light and inflated like a balloon. If someone was going to die that's how it would happen. His brain would burst. That would be something worth telling your friends.

And I wonder if that's why I don't dread death now – because I can't imagine it as vividly as I did when I was a child. The only thing I am sure of is that it will make a good story. Hey guys, guess what happened to me!

Six

When I worked in Manchester near the Royal Infirmary, I walked past a billboard every day which said: *30% of everyone who reads this will get cancer.*

That always puzzled me. Of all the hundreds, maybe thousands of people I had met I only ever heard of two or three of them having cancer. Could that really be true, I thought? So many? Is that really what's waiting for one in three of us?

At that time cancer meant tumours, of course, which were always described as the size of a golf ball, or a grapefruit. They were monstrous things that grew inside the body and broke up and spread through its fibres like spores. They erupted through skin and left black craters and lagoons of rotten flesh.

Diseases of the blood were very different things. If I thought of someone having leukaemia, I pictured them lying with pale skin on white pillows, wrapped in white sheets. They were already ghostlike, falling away from life quietly. I could imagine myself doing that. I still can.

So when I first heard the words blood cancer, I assumed it wasn't a real thing. How can there be tumours in the blood? Where is its rotten core? I thought people who said they had blood cancer were just looking for a more exciting way to describe their listless bodies.

Seven

On Sunday morning my brother called.

Hi. Where are you?

I'm in Poundland buying batteries.

Give me a ring when you get home.

I knew straight away what had happened. Half an hour later I called him back.

Mum passed away in the night.

Yes, I guessed.

Four o'clock this morning, the nurse said. There was no one with her.

And I could only think of her lying in the dark, frightened and alone. I didn't cry for her death, but for her fear.

Eight

I didn't realise how nervous the doctor was until I asked him to write down the name of my disease. I knew I would never remember it otherwise.

His hand was shaking. He wrote a word. Crossed it out. Wrote it again. Checked his screen. Wrote it a third time.

I looked at the crooked letters, the long string of syllables, thinking How can I even say that?

Nine

It must have been after eleven when they took me to surgery. I was either in a wheelchair or on a bed. It's hard to remember. The hospital was empty at that time of night, the lights dimmed and the corridors cold.

But the room was brightly lit with a harsh fluorescence. Two people were waiting, both masked, one a man the other a woman – the familiar complement of doctor and nurse. I was either laid out or sat up for the procedure. Again I'm not sure. I didn't feel the incision under my collar bone either, but I knew that the liquid trickling down my side was blood.

An X-ray machine was placed above my chest and if I turned my head to the right I could see the picture on the screen, the tube piercing the vein and pushing down through its narrow channel. I didn't look, of course, I never do, but the quiet voice of the doctor told me what was happening.

Then a thin plastic collar was fixed under the ripped flap of skin, which he sewed around it. All I felt was the tug of the thread pulling me together again.

Back in the ward I could see what they had given me – plastic tubes protruding from my chest like the tentacles of a sea creature. The Hickman Line. I worried that they might snag in my sleep and tear from my body, so the nurse taped them to my skin. Ten days later the tubes were removed, hastily, in another late-night operation. There was an infection, I was told – candida – and I imagined a frothing yeast gathering inside me like spawn.

For months afterwards the nurses taking blood would say, 'Have you got a line in?' But all I had left was the inky mark of the tape on my chest that I couldn't wash away.

Ten

On my third day in the isolation ward, the chemo kicked in hard. I was warned it would happen. First there was a raging thirst, then my skin reddened and rose up in welts and pustules across my stomach and legs. The young doctor – I think he was young behind his mask and gown – lifted the sheet, shuddered and said, 'Bless you.' Then my phone pinged.

After the doctor and nurses left I checked the WhatsApp message. It was from Alastair:

> *Hi. How are you doing? Send me your list of desert island discs.*

This was easy, as he knew it would be. I'd had them prepared for a long time: start with *All the Young Dudes* and *Drive-in Saturday*, then work my way through the years to *Bitches Brew*. I sent him the list and added:

> *You know I've told them I'm not going on the show unless they play the whole of every song.*

Next morning I could hardly talk. I lay sweating and twitching in bed. There was a drip in my arm feeding me potassium, magnesium, all the trace elements I'd lost. More masked nurses came and went. Another message from Alastair:

Who are your top ten guitarists?

This was harder. There was Bill Nelson, obviously, then probably George Benson. After that I ran out of energy and ideas.

You know I'm not very interested in guitarists.

Overnight my body bloated. There was a stone's weight of water in my feet and knees. I spent hours pissing into bottles, weeping with the pain. The nurses brought liquid morphine and cups of tea.

OK an easy one. Top ten films?

Every morning there was another message, which he must have sent over breakfast before going to work. By the time all my hair fell out two weeks later I had replied with the best footballers of all time, top ten sitcoms, American actors, Clash songs and all the shared enthusiasms of our youth.

The only person who was allowed to visit was Julie, and she came to sit with me every day wearing a surgical mask, gloves and gown. When I couldn't talk, or just fell asleep, she would stay and read for hours. She was always there when I woke up. One day she said:

It's a pity Alastair couldn't come and see you.

Yes, but he sends me messages every day.

Oh, good. What does he have to say?

He asks me to send him lists. All sorts of things – music, football, films.

Why does he do that?

I think it's how old friends show they love each other.

Eleven

Let's call her Angela. I don't know her real name and probably never will, but Angela is a good name considering all she did for me.

How much do I know? She was nineteen years old then, which means that she'll be twenty-four now. She lived in Wales, but probably doesn't any more. I imagine she has blond hair, slightly wavy or curly, shoulder length, pale skin and a round smiling face.

She's a student, I'm guessing. Or she was, five years ago. An arts subject, judging from her handwriting on the card she sent with its large looping letters in pale blue ink. She probably played sport in a university team, netball or hockey, just for fun on Wednesday afternoons. Maybe it was there that she saw a campaign for people to register as stem cell donors. It was such an easy thing to do. Most of the team did the same.

When the letter came, saying that she was a match for someone, her mam was worried but she reassured her. 'It won't hurt', she told her. 'And it will help to save a life. Why wouldn't I do it?'

So she made her donation, finished her course and moved to England. She's starting her career in marketing now, thinking about getting married and hoping to buy a flat with her boyfriend. Too young yet to have children, she tells her friends, but maybe one day.

And as she thinks about the future, where she could travel and what she might do, she wonders about the man she gave her blood and stem cells to. Is he still alive? Where does he live? What is that part of her body doing now, somewhere out there in the world?

Twelve

The staff nurse marched into the room playing an imaginary trumpet.

I thought we should have a fanfare!

Two other nurses followed her. One pushed a flat metal trolley with the usual array of swabs and bottles. The other carried a plastic bag containing a pale orange coloured liquid. She held it like an offering, shifting its weight from hand to hand to keep it moving, to make sure it stayed fluid.

So this is the stuff that's going to save my life?

Yes, freshly delivered this morning.

How long will it take to go in?

Oh, about twenty minutes.

The staff nurse set up the bag on the IV stand, inserted a tube into the nozzle at the bottom and attached the other end to the cannula in my wrist.

That's it, ready to go.

She turned on the tap, flicked the tube with her finger.

Twenty minutes and you're done.

We watched the bag as it emptied its contents into me. Twenty minutes. A trumpet. A fanfare. A gift.

Taxis Derma:
an arrangement of skin

The first dead animal I ever saw was a black dog that had been hit by a car. It might have been a labrador but in those days so many dogs on the streets were mongrels you could never be sure. A white Ford Anglia had stopped near our house and a woman stood next to it with a handkerchief in her hand, dabbing at her eyes. The dog lay on its side. Drips of blood fell from its nose and made a thick red pool on the tarmac. When its chest stopped rising and falling someone unfolded a newspaper and placed it gently over its head.

The dog must have belonged to someone but very few of us had pets. Maybe a goldfish from the fair or a cageful of white mice in the outhouse. But there was a nature room in the local museum and when we were eight or nine years old we went there during the school holidays to take our shoes off and slide around on the polished wooden floor. The other boys would dare each other to look at the solitary human skeleton, but I was more interested in the animals and birds in glass cases that lined the walls.

There were no exotic creatures that I remember, but I had never seen foxes, weasels or badgers before, or the waders and seabirds in their glassy pools. I loved the birds of prey, the kestrels and buzzards perched on branches, and one big white owl with its wings spread wider than I could reach. Every single one of them had its eyes open, which seemed very strange to me. Did they never go to sleep?

**

I hadn't thought about these things for years but when I came north to work, my office in the county archive was next to a museum which had a big natural history collection. Occasionally I'd walk through its ground floor galleries, looking at the exhibits as I went to buy a sandwich from the café. One lunchtime I heard a voice near a display of local wildlife:

'Well, my beauty, where did you wander off to last night? Looking for bugs and worms, eh? I know you well enough, my lad.'

The old man saw me watching and smiled up at me. 'What do you think of him? My beauty?'

He nodded towards a badger which stood mid-shuffle, one shoulder slightly raised and its nose tilted towards a smell in the distance.

'It's very lifelike,' I said, looking around the room. 'More than some of the others here.'

'He's one of mine, that's why.'

'How do you mean, yours?'

'I settled him.'

'You made it?'

'You don't make something like this, man. You prepare him, you mount him, but you don't make him. He makes himself.'

'You're a taxidermist?'

'I used to work here, looking after all these,' he said, waving his hand towards the exhibits. 'And I settled some of them. I just come back to see them now, to make sure these people know what they're doing.'

'And do they?'

'No, they don't listen to a word I say.'

I gestured that I needed to go, looked at my watch and started to move away. He had already turned back to the case and was peering under a fox's head, tutting and sighing. As I walked to the door, I saw one of the museum managers I recognised from a Council Health and Safety meeting. He nodded as I passed him.

'I see you've been collared by Les,' he said.

'He told me he used to work here.'

'Mm. And now he can't keep away. He's a bloody nuisance, to be honest.'

*

Over the next few weeks I went to the museum more often in my breaks from work. The Roman artefacts and old pots didn't interest me, but I was always drawn to the animals, birds and reptiles. Some of them looked worn and beaten down, but there were others that had a life about them that I couldn't understand. What was it that animated them and pulled me close? I found that it was better not to face up to them directly, to interrogate them. They felt more alive when you came alongside them and looked out to see the world as they saw it, even if the view was no more than a monotonous row of display cases and tiled floors.

Les was there more often than not, but he didn't pay any attention to me. He was usually talking to one of the attendants. I could hear him from the other side of the gallery.

'I told them what would happen. Look, that poor bugger's suffering.' He pointed at a stoat which was listing to one side. 'Nobody's doing anything about it, are they?'

'I can't do anything,' the man replied. 'Listen, Les, if you carry on like this you're going to get thrown out. I heard the security guys talking. You're really asking for trouble, you know.'

He walked away muttering and I followed him towards the door.

'Les,' I said. 'Sorry, do you mind? I wanted to ask you something.'

He turned and screwed his eyes at me. 'What have I done now?'

'It's OK. I don't work here. You told me about your badger the other day.'

'Oh, yeah. I remember. You could see the life in him. I could tell.'

Outside the building he pointed to a bench near the entrance and we sat down together in the shade.

'So what do you want to know?'

'I just wondered, how did you get to be a taxidermist?'

'Well, let's see. I started out as a miner... Don't look so surprised. I might not seem much now but I was a strong bastard when I was young. I could shift coal with the best of them.'

He told me how he worked in a local colliery when he left school, but preferred being out in the fields and woods, watching birds and following the trails of animals – the deer, badgers and foxes near his home. He came into the city when he could to visit the library and museum, learning things about nature they never taught him in the classroom. The old museum taxidermist took a shine to him and offered to teach him what he knew, and eventually he was taken on as a junior in the conservation department.

'And I spent nearly forty years here until they cleared me out like old rubbish. I asked who would do my job when I was gone and they told me it would be 'outsourced'. Which means that no one does it. It's going to hell in a handbasket, and that saying comes from the mines too.'

*

I met Les quite often after that and sometimes we'd share a sandwich for lunch in the park near the museum. He was always keen to talk, full of passion, particularly when he explained how you prepare an animal or a bird, how you remove the skin from its frame of bone, build an armature, mount it, settle it in position. He had settled hundreds, he said, and even though they were mostly museum pieces he spoke about them as though they were still living things. I asked him once how he could think of them in that way, after he had taken their bodies apart with his own hands.

'Use your imagination, man,' he said. 'You dream your dreams and so do they. And when you're dead you'll have a long time to remember what it's like to be alive.'

*

I had always thought I enjoyed my job, but after talking to Les I began to see myself surrounded only by dead things. I felt like a morgue attendant at work and at home. In the archive I catalogued papers and documents which were important to other people but their stories didn't move me. My house was full of antiques that I'd picked up in shops and flea markets. I never bought expensive pieces but I always looked out for things that seemed lost and in need of a home. I thought that I was doing something positive but I might as well have buried them.

One Sunday afternoon I went to an antiques fair in Corbridge, as I often did on quiet weekends, just to look around. I was picking through a pile of old tools and tin boxes when I glanced up and saw a pair of brown eyes looking at me from a shelf behind the stall. Then a fox's black nose, white whiskers and broad head pushed toward me as though it had asked a question and was waiting for an answer. I knew straight away that I had to have it, which is always a mistake in a place like that. The sellers know when you really want something and then there's no point in trying to haggle. I ended up paying the asking price, which was more than I could afford, and left quickly, back to my car, holding him steady on his wooden base.

At home I tried to clean the fox as much as I dared, carefully brushing the dust from his paws, his muzzle and along his sleek back. He had obviously been neglected and I was afraid to disturb his tail for fear of doing any damage. Then I set him down in the living room, near the fire, but not too close, to bring some warmth to his old fur. And we sat together quietly, watching the evening sky go dark and waiting for the shadows outside to blacken under the hedges.

*

I was keen to see Les again, to tell him what I had bought, but also because I needed his help. In the light of day it was obvious that the fox was in a worse condition than I thought. His body was unsteady and a seam behind his rear leg was coming apart. There were doubtless other problems that I couldn't see.

I was sure Les could help, but he wasn't keen at first.

'What did you want to buy something like that for?' he said. 'It's probably a bit of tat put together by an amateur. I've seen too many of those in my time.'

But eventually he agreed to take a look at the fox, and told me to take it to his place near High Spen, just a few miles from where I lived. He'd need his tools, he said.

When I arrived at the row of old miners' cottages, he took me round the back to his workshop which he had set up in a large shed. I was surprised at how well equipped it was, with a stainless-steel bench, two freezers and rows of equipment set out in racks on the wall. A few small animals and birds in various stages of repair stood on the shelves.

'I still do some work for friends and rich folk who know no better,' he said. 'They pay well so they can display their trophies.'

'You've got a lot of gear here.' I said as I looked around.

'Most of these tools are from the museum. I shamed them into letting me have them when I left. They didn't even know how much they were worth, the stupid sods.'

I handed him the crate I had brought with me. He took the fox out and put it on his workbench.

'Oh, you poor little bugger,' he said, as he pressed into its fur with his thick fingers. 'Well, I've seen worse. Leave him with me, I'm sure we can sort him out.'

As I left he was bent over the bench, gently coaxing him, easing him with his quiet words.

*

When I went back a week later I couldn't believe it was the same creature. My fox had been cleaned up as I expected, but he seemed more alert, more vital than before. It was hard to tell what exactly had changed. He was a little more upright, but there was also more of a purpose in its stance. His body had a slight turn, one of his rear legs pushed back, and his head lifted up, listening. I asked Les what he had done.

'Just performed my magic,' he said. 'I waited and I watched and saw which way he wanted to go. Then I opened him up and adjusted the armature a bit. It didn't need much. He was almost there. That's probably what you saw in him when you found him.'

'You've brought him to life, Les.'

'Everything that lives is holy. You just have to pay it proper respect.'

I must have looked puzzled. What was he talking about? Holy?

'William Blake,' he said. 'You should read more books. You know where the library is, don't you?'

As he put the fox back in his crate, I asked Les how much I owed him.

'Nothing for this one. You can do me a favour some time.'

The fox looked so much better when I took him home. He stood in my lounge, on the floor near the sofa where he could see the small garden outside. I sat with him most evenings, just the two of us enjoying the silence. Every day I looked forward to getting home from work so I could spend time with my new companion.

*

At weekends I started to travel out to other places where I knew there were antiques shops and markets. My visits were more purposeful now, as I searched out other animals instead of the odds and ends I used to pick through. And there were more of them than I expected, usually tucked away in back rooms and dusty corners. Foxes and small birds were easy to find, and I took home a couple that caught my eye. The real prizes were a tawny owl and a beautiful otter that I had to haggle hard over. I learned to hide my enthusiasm and shrug nonchalantly when I saw them, even when they urged me to pick them up quickly and rush away.

Les began to get used to my calls. Every couple of weeks I took something new to his workshop and he told me straight away if I was wasting his time.

'This one is long past dead,' he said more than once. 'If you paid money for that, you're a fool. Just go and put it in the ground somewhere.'

But it was obvious when he saw something he liked, something he knew he could work with. Then he'd become very quiet, his hands would start caressing, probing and pushing, and he'd mutter under his breath, words I could barely hear.

'Oh, you're a beauty, aren't you. Let's see if we can help you fly. Yes, you're going to be alright, lovely one.'

I left him then. He wasn't going to talk to me any more. All I could do was go home and wait for him to let me know when he had done.

*

Near where I lived, just on the edge of town, was a large wood where I walked on summer evenings and at weekends when I wasn't out looking for animals and birds to bring home. The main paths were usually busy with walkers and mountain bikes but in the deeper, older wood it was quiet and I could spend hours there without seeing anyone. One Sunday I glanced at my fox as I was putting my boots on. He sat in his usual place looking out, stretching towards the garden. The question he had asked me when I first saw him seemed more urgent now, and without even thinking what I was doing, I picked him up, put him in a box from the garage and carried him out with me.

Once we had gone over the bridge at the edge of the fields, we headed up through the trees towards the higher ground. Half a mile further on was a deep ravine that led back down into the river valley. I had been there once before and knew how difficult it was to climb down, and even harder to find a way out. At the bottom of the slope, where the river widens and slows, I opened the box and set the fox down under a bank of earth which was shaded with grass and ferns. I pointed his eager nose towards the water, covered his wooden base with soil and leaves and left him there, half-hidden in the undergrowth.

*

I was trying to avoid Les. I kept away from the museum where I was most likely to see him, but he found me anyway. As I left the office one day by the back door, heading towards the car park, he walked towards me with a big grin on his face.

'You're a mad bugger, aren't you?'

'Hello, Les. What's up?' I said, although I already knew what he meant.

'Don't forget, I know those woods better than you. Better than anyone probably. I saw the otter first, and it didn't take me long to find the others.'

'Sorry, Les. I know you worked hard on them, but I had to do it. I don't know why. I just had to.'

'You were listening to them. I've never seen anything so fucking crazy, but it sort of makes sense. Don't worry, I haven't disturbed them. Well, only the owl. She wasn't going to last long where you left her. The first strong wind would bring her down, so I put her in a hollow and used stronger twine. She'll be fine now.'

He was still grinning, and I was red with shame. To hear him say that he understood what I had done just made me feel more pathetic. I shrugged and started to walk away.

'Wait. I need a favour from you,' he said. He pointed over towards the museum. 'My badger. I need to get him out of there and you can do it for me.'

*

Les had a plan and I couldn't escape it. He wanted me to steal the badger for him. He said it was rightly his anyway, he had settled it, and besides I owed him. What could I do? I tried to explain how risky it was, that my job was on the line if I got caught, but he pushed all that aside.

'It'll be easy,' he said, 'I have at least one friend left in there, and he'll make sure the cabinet is open. All you need to do is go in and take it. I'll keep the others busy. You just walk in.'

'Les,' I said, 'this is mad. What about the cctv?'

'I told you, man, they don't care anymore. They won't even notice it's gone. By the time they do, the tapes will be wiped over.'

I knew there was nothing I could say or do to get out of it. The damned badger was telling me as well as Les.

*

We arranged to meet on Wednesday afternoon, at a quiet time near to closing. I left work early with a large archive box under my arm, walked across the road and through the front door of the museum. In my work suit and tie, and with a Council ID

29

on a lanyard around my neck, I looked as inconspicuous as anyone passing through the building. As soon as I opened the door to the gallery on the ground floor, I heard shouting from the far corner. Les was haranguing the attendant and a security guard who had come out of one of the back rooms. I had never seen him so furious, waving his arms and ranting as they tried to move him towards the rear door. I walked over to the badger's cabinet, opened the front and lifted him into my box. In his place I left a small piece of card Les had given me:

European Badger (Meles meles)
Removed for Conservation

He was waiting for me in the car park behind the council offices.

'I don't think we'll be going back there for a while,' he laughed, rubbing his hands together. 'I've been barred, they said. Fucking barred!'

I handed the box to him, but he pushed it back at me.

'No, you take him. You know where he belongs, and I'll find him easy enough. Don't worry. I know exactly where he'll be.'

When I had closed the boot of my car, Les reached out to shake my hand.

'What are you going to do now?' he said. 'Your place must be pretty empty these days. Back to the antiques shops?'

'No,' I said, 'I've finished with that. I was thinking of getting a dog for company. A labrador probably. A black one.'

'Do you need my help?'

'What? Could you?'

'Yeah, of course I could. There's a man over in Wylam owes me a favour.'

The Notebook

Jamie held the notebook under the table so that no one would see it if they walked by. He turned it over in his hand, and ran his fingers over its soft cover, as he watched the door at the end of the carriage in case the woman came back.

She had stepped onto the train just in front of him in Warrington and sat on the other side of the aisle. At that time in the morning she looked like any other business traveller on her way to a meeting, but instead of taking out a laptop or phone she put a notebook and pencil next to her takeaway coffee. He glanced over at her occasionally as he read through his emails and each time she was looking out of the window. Once or twice she opened her notebook and wrote a few words then closed it again. She wasn't particularly attractive or striking in any way, at least Jamie didn't think so at the time. It was her calmness that caught his attention, her absorption in something that he couldn't see, and he kept looking her way to see if she would do anything to disturb the still air around her.

As the train passed Edge Hill, just a few minutes from Lime Street, she took her bag from the luggage rack and walked along the carriage. She didn't hurry and Jamie assumed she just wanted to get to the door before everyone else. He noticed straight away that the notebook was lying on her seat but he hesitated for a second, not sure if he should call after her. Instead he reached across the aisle and picked it up. It wasn't heavy but it felt surprisingly solid and real in his hand. Like something he might want to keep. He had to get off as well, so he slipped it into the side pocket of his briefcase and eased into the queue of people leaving the train. The platform was busy as everyone crowded at the ticket barrier and he looked to see if she was there. If he spotted her he could give the notebook back, he thought, but he was relieved that she had gone.

At the office he kept his door closed. He pushed papers around on his desk and ignored the phone when it rang. The image of the woman on the train wouldn't leave him. He wondered where she was going and what she might be doing now. Perhaps she worked at something creative. He imagined her walking through the long rooms of the Walker Gallery, or sitting in the back row of a rehearsal at the Philharmonic Hall. He could see her writing, correcting drafts, climbing the stairs at a publisher's to discuss the outline of a new novel.

Next day he looked out for her at the station. He sat in the same carriage as before, in the same seat, but she wasn't there. Her notebook was still in his briefcase. He might have been tempted once or twice to take it out and look at it, but he preferred just knowing that he had it with him. He tried to reconstruct the scene from the previous journey, turning slightly in his seat so that he could glance across the aisle without being conspicuous. He saw her looking out of the window, gazing across the fields then opening the notebook and writing, just a few words at a time. She lifted her cup, pushed her hair back from her face, took a sip of her coffee, rolled the pencil across the table with the tips of her fingers.

By the end of the week, Jamie had made up a complete story for the woman: her riverside home, her tastes in food and films, the art on her walls and quiet evenings listening to Bach cantatas. He thought about cold water swimming, but decided against it. Yoga and meditation fitted perfectly, at a Mediterranean retreat with white buildings, olive trees and the blue sea behind her. And in every scene he imagined, in everything she did, she was alone. He couldn't move beyond the singularity of her. No, the truth is that he didn't want to add anyone else, to take her away from her impeccable solitude.

Then on Monday she reappeared. He was in his usual seat, so preoccupied with his thoughts that he didn't notice her come into the carriage. She sat a little further away than before, and after the train had been moving for a few minutes he glanced up and saw her. She was looking straight at him and caught his eye for just a second before turning away. He opened his laptop and kept his head down for the rest of the journey.

When they reached Liverpool he followed her as she walked out onto Skelhorne Street. He wanted to talk to her, but what could he say? How could he explain himself? They walked towards the taxi rank and, despite the crowds, she must have sensed that someone was behind her. She stopped and turned around. He took the notebook from his briefcase and held it out.

'I think this is yours,' he said. 'You left it on the train last week.'

She looked down at the book in his hand and he added quickly, 'I haven't read it. Really.'

Then she did something that he could never have imagined and had very rarely seen – she raised one eyebrow to a high arch while holding his gaze – and took it from him without a word.

She turned and waited at the edge of the pavement. When a taxi arrived she picked up her bag, took a step to one side and dropped the notebook into a rubbish bin on the kerb. It hit the bottom with a hollow thud and Jamie could only stand and watch as she got into the cab and drove away.

List of Lies

At a ferry terminal on the south coast of England, several young people sit in an office on the upper floor of a portacabin. They are taking bookings for ferry crossings and holiday cottages in France. It's early summer in the late 1980s and all of this is real but nothing is true.

***

Steve puts the phone down and sits back in his chair, eyes wide and cheeks puffed out like a blowfish.

'What's up?' Andy says. 'It was only a number three, wasn't it?'

'Yeah, but you won't believe who I was talking to. When I asked for the name on his booking he said, Saltram, Lord Saltram.'

'Maybe you should have dropped a number four on him then,' Andy laughs.

'But I didn't sign up to tell lies to people like that.'

'Anyone can be a lord these days,' Andy says. 'You just have to pay enough money or suck enough cock. Oops, 'scuse me Rachel,' he nods to the young woman sitting opposite who bares her teeth at him.

'Not that one.' Dylan looks over the partition between the desks. 'The Saltrams go back to the fourteenth century. In the Civil War they...'

'Oh, shut up, loser. We might have known you'd have something to say.'

'Just trying to educate you, Andy. You should be grateful.' Dylan carries on writing, pressing his pen hard through the carbon sheets in the tickets.

Steve picks up the booking chart for August and runs his finger down the list of gîtes in Brittany, then checks the cards slotted into a rack on the wall behind him. God, another double booking. Another one to cancel. He glances at a piece of paper tucked under the glass top of the desk. His list of lies.

Number 1 – Gîte destroyed by fire

Number 2 – Owner died

Number 3 – Subsidence

Number 4... yes, maybe he should have used Number 4 – Sewage overflow.

*

The staffroom is empty when Steve walks in, which is just as well. It isn't much bigger than a cupboard with space for a vending machine, three plastic chairs and a small window overlooking the dock. He presses a button and gazes out as the drink sputters into a cup behind him. The oily harbour water rolls against the sea wall in the wake of the last ferry to leave. It will be near the breakwater by now and on its way to France. Full of happy families, if they're lucky and it doesn't run aground in Roscoff again. While he watches, a dark shadow moves under the surface of the water then slips downwards out of sight. He shakes his head and winces at the thought of all the angry phone calls and letters of complaint.

He picks the plastic cup from under the nozzle, and as he takes a first scalding sip he hears footsteps along the corridor. You can't creep up on anyone in a portacabin and he knows who it is from the clip of her heels.

'Hi, Rachel,' he calls out, before she reaches the door.

'I thought I'd find you in here. Are you alright?'

'Oh yes, it's just the same old crap, isn't it? Double bookings, cancellations, tickets lost in the post.'

He smiles. She smiles back. Her big, open smile. They're still friends.

At the party in Andy's flat at the weekend he almost kissed her. Or she almost kissed him, he isn't sure which. They were sitting on the floor talking, with their backs against a sofa, and found themselves leaning towards each other. Close enough to smell the wine on her breath. Then what happened? Oh, yes, Mandy walked in and he saw her looking over and grinning at them. He was relieved then, and even more relieved now. He doesn't know how he'd be able to sit opposite Rachel at work every day if he'd leaned just a little further.

'What's that you're drinking?' she says, with a grimace. 'It's not the soup, is it?'

'It's hot lemon. It's the only one that doesn't taste of fish.'

'Don't be daft. It'll ruin your teeth, though.'

He runs his tongue around his mouth, feeling the gritty residue from the drink rough against his gums. 'You're right. I'm disintegrating. It'll wear me away if this place doesn't do it first.'

*

'How come she gets away with it every day,' Steve whispers, nodding towards Elaine who sits at an empty desk in the corner picking at her nails. She's small and red-headed. Fierce looking. He doesn't speak to her unless he has to. She sees him talking and stares back until he turns away.

'She's permanent,' Andy says, 'so she gets the easy jobs. You know how it works.'

'All she does is put vouchers into envelopes. Why have I got the bloody gîtes?'

'Because you're a smart alec,' Andy says. 'We all saw how you carried on in training: *Yes, Elise. No Elise. I've memorised all the ferry timetables, Elise.* You got the hard job because you asked for it.'

Steve looks down the corridor to Elise's office. The interview three months before, in a room thick with her cigarette smoke and perfume, was his first after A Levels. She introduced herself, leaning forward over the desk to shake his hand. He can't remember anything she asked or anything he said in reply, but he does remember how many buttons of her blouse were undone. Was that deliberate? Was he supposed to look or not look? He must have done well enough despite blushing and stuttering because she offered him a season's contract until the end of the summer. Maybe, he wondered as he walked away from the ferry terminal that day, thinking of her buttons and the lacy outline of her bra, maybe it's because she's French?

'Tell you what I heard, though.' Andy is whispering as well now. 'Richard in baggage told me. At the staff party at the end of last season, she went into her office with two of the crew off the Santander boat. Sam walked in and saw them. One of them with his trousers round his ankles, the other on his knees with his head between her legs.'

'No way.'

'That's what I heard. Stick around 'til the end of the season, one of us might get lucky.'

'She's old enough to be my mother.'

'So?' Andy raises his eyebrows at him.

'In your dreams, sailor boy,' Dylan's voice comes over the partition.

'This is a private conversation, if you don't mind. You shouldn't be listening.'

'I wasn't listening, but you start squeaking when you get excited.'

Steve opens his desk drawer and picks up a thick pile of query forms. Most of them have been there for weeks. Every one a problem, every one another painful phone call. He drops them again. No, he'll look at them later, maybe another day. When he's thought up a few more additions for his long list of lies.

'If anyone wants me,' he says, 'I'll be on the telex.'

*

He rattles down the metal staircase to the main concourse. In the distance he can hear the crowds queueing for ticket checks, the noise of their voices rising like waves as the terminal doors open and close. The Roscoff ferry is ready for boarding in the outer dock and its white bulk looms over the harbour wall. He peers at the water. There's that black shape again, just under the surface, brushing against its hull.

As he walks into the ticket office he stops and looks over to the third desk by the window, to Mandy's desk, to see if she's there. She is, and his pulse, as he knew it would, jumps slightly.

The people around her are on their phones, checking ferry charts, scribbling notes, taking bookings. Only Mandy looks relaxed and unhurried. She leans back as she talks to her caller, with her long fingers combing through her hair. Steve was told that she has the best sales figures in the company and he asked once how she did it.

'It's easy,' she said. 'You just listen, work out what they want and promise it to them.'

'Like what?'

'If someone asks 'Does that cabin have a shower?' you say 'Yes, of course it does'. If they want to know if the hotel has a pool, you say 'Oh yes, one large pool and a small one for the children.' Her voice was low and soft and he understood completely why she always made the sale.

'What if there isn't a shower or a pool?' he asked.

She smiled and shook her head. 'That's not my problem anymore, is it?'

Mandy, he thinks as he gazes at her, you could tell me all the lies in the world and I'd believe every one of them.

*

Tucking himself into a corner near the post room, Steve sits down in front of the telex machine. He puts his list of gîte bookings onto the document stand and presses Next Message. The printer shudders then settles into a rumbling purr. It reminds him of the sound of the small launches in the harbour and if he wasn't so nervous he might find it relaxing. But then, he thinks, if he had been given any training he wouldn't be nervous at all. Instead Elise put a sheet of instructions in his hand and said, 'It's just like typing. You know how to type, don't you, Steve?'

'Yes, of course. No problem,' he lied. Well, maybe not quite a lie this time, just a small exaggeration.

Words flicker across the narrow screen, one letter at a time, as he pokes at the keyboard with two rigid fingers. Only three lines of text are visible and he has to keep scrolling backwards and forwards to make sure the names of the gîtes line up with the correct booking dates. He knows that any mistakes will find their way back to him sooner or later. Even when Rachel brings him a drink at break time he barely looks up to say thank you.

Eventually the last page is turned over and the typing finished. He rubs at his sore knuckles. How long did that take? An hour, an hour and a half? He presses the Print button, and the perforated tape containing the telex message spools out of the back of the printer. He checks the instructions again and feeds the tape into a slot in the front of the machine, dials the connecting number, and presses Send. Then he sits back and stretches as it chunters through to the office in France.

'There, easy, no problem at all,' he says as he picks the long trail of tape off the floor, tears it into pieces and drops it into the bin at his side. He's wondering if Mandy will still be at her desk when the phone next to the telex rings.

'Is that Steve?' a French voice asks. 'Are you still there, at the telex?'

'Yes, Steve here.'

'This is Didier in St Malo. I have received a message from you.'

'Bonjour, Didier. Yes, I just sent it.'

'It is all wrong, Steve. Gibberish, you would say.'

'What do you mean?'

'It makes no sense. You put the tape in the wrong way round, didn't you?'

*

Back in the office, Steve slumps onto his desk.

'Bloody telex! I hate it. It would be easier to read the bookings out over the phone.'

'You could do it in French. With your A Level and all. They'd love that,' Andy says. 'Anyway, I heard it's all going to be computerised next season.'

'You don't think I'll still be here, do you?'

'Some of us will. I'm going to apply to be made permanent. I know a guy at the Poly who's got a computer in his workshop. He plays games all day and he can even get Fiesta and Men Only on it.'

Steve glances over towards Rachel's desk. 'You can't do that here.'

'Well, you won't be here to know, will you?" Andy says as he walks away grinning.

Dylan waves his fist up and down at him as he passes his desk.

'Dylan?' Steve says. 'Why do you hate him so much?'

'I don't hate him. I feel sorry for him.'

'How come?'

'Don't you know? He was in the merchant navy. He joined up straight from school, all set to sail the world, meet the girls, live the life.'

'So what happened?'

'He got sea sick before he reached the channel. He managed three trips, and was ill on all of them. They gave him the push and he ended up here, where he'll stay forever if he can, jacking off and generally being an idiot.'

'He hates you, though,' Steve says.

'Yeah, that's true. Can you believe we were friends at school?'

'You went to university, though, didn't you?'

'I studied history, for all the good it did me,' Dylan says. 'And now I'm back here as well. And he hates me for it.'

'Why?'

'He told me once, when he was drunk. He said, 'You had all the chances, and you wasted them'.'

'Did you waste them?'

Dylan sits back, and waves his hand over his desk, at the pens and brochures and ferry tickets scattered across it, and at the charts and timetables pinned to the wall.

*

The racks are getting fuller every day – hotels and B&Bs along one wall, gîtes on the other behind Steve's desk. As the phone calls come in and forms arrive in the post he writes out booking cards and puts them in the plastic slots, one for each gîte through every week of the summer.

Andy hops in behind him and drops two cards into the rack.

'What's that, Andy?' he says.

'Another booking for you. Pluherlin. 28th of July for two weeks.'

'But I'm holding the second week for someone else. Look, it's there in pending.'

'I just took it on the phone. It's a firm booking.'

'For Christ's sake, Andy. You know you can't confirm a booking until you check pending.' Steve looks around the office. 'Everyone knows that, don't they?' he says loudly. There are a few murmurs from the far end of the room. Rachel nods at him as she heads to the door. Dylan keeps his head down, Elaine's chair is empty.

Steve takes the cards out of their slots and throws them on his desk. 'Another sodding double booking. For Chrissakes!' He picks up a query form from the pile by his phone, scribbles a note and drops it in the drawer with the rest.

'I'm on a break,' he says, glaring at Andy as he walks out.

He has just stepped into the staffroom and is about to get a drink when he hears doors banging and heavy feet hurrying up the stairs and along the corridor. Two men in green overalls rush past with bags in their hands. Before he has time to look outside Rachel appears at the door, her face white and her eyes wet with tears.

'What's happening, Rach?' he says.

'It's Elaine. One of the cleaners found her in the toilets.'

He puts his arm around her as she sobs into a handkerchief. Then they walk back to the office where people are already standing around talking.

'Somebody said something about pills.' Andy says.

'Her husband left her last week,' Rachel sniffs. 'She was in a real state.'

'Wow. I didn't even know she was married.'

'You wouldn't know, would you?' she shouts. 'When did any of you even bloody talk to her?'

*

Lunchtime is nearly over. Steve walks into the canteen and looks around but he can't see anyone he knows. A woman near the till is putting away trays and wiping down the counter.

'Have you got anything left, Grace?' he says.

'Just a couple of pasties.'

'Go on, I'll have one. And what's that?' he asks, pointing at a metal dish simmering under a hot bulb.

'Tinned tomatoes from breakfast'

'Some of that as well, then.'

She drops a pasty onto the middle of a plate and pours the tomatoes around it.

He hands her 80p and carries his tray to a table near a window in the corner. As he picks up his knife he sees Mandy at the entrance. She raises her hand, glances at the empty counter, and starts to walk over. Oh, thank you lord, he thinks. Thank you.

'Hi, Mandy,' he says, trying to keep his voice steady. 'Did you hear about Elaine?'

'Elaine?'

'From upstairs in our office. The ambulance.'

'Oh, god, yeah. Terrible,' she says as she searches through her bag. 'I'm just on a quick break. I need to keep my bookings up.'

She opens a tin of Old Holborn and pulls strands of tobacco onto a Rizla. Steve's knife and fork hover over his plate as he watches her roll up and lick slowly along the edge of the paper.

'You've always got a lot of bookings,' he says.

'Yeah, but I'm leaving at the end of the month so I'm trying to hit the bonus again before I go.'

'Leaving? Where are you going?'

'Down to Spain first, then over to Morocco. I've been told about a place there where they grow the best hash.'

'Mandy...'

She flips the top of her lighter and turns to blow smoke away from him. 'Mmm?'

'Let me come with you. I'm going to leave as well. I can go to Morocco with you.'

'How old are you, Steve?' she smiles. 'Anyway, I thought you were going to university.'

'I don't know. Maybe not, or I can do it next year.'

'I'm going with Nick and a couple of friends. In his van.'

'Nick? The Irish guy at Andy's party?'

'Yes, Nick. My boyfriend.'

Nick. The Irish guy. The one with tattoos. And a van. He looks like Rory Gallagher and probably plays guitar as well. Bloody hell. Steve looks over Mandy's shoulder, and as he stares out at the dockside two thick tentacles curl over the

49

edge of the wharf and wrap themselves around the railing. They tense then fall back, leaving a slick black trail behind them.

'That looks like something's been murdered,' Mandy says, pointing her cigarette at the doughy red slop on his plate. Steve cringes and thinks of the ambulance again. She opens a paper bag and holds it across to him. 'Here, have some of these.'

'What is it?'

'Mushrooms.' She picks one out and puts it in her mouth. 'They might make your afternoon more interesting.'

He looks out at the inky slime on the dock, dripping off the wall into the water.

'Thanks,' he says, 'but I really don't think I need them.'

*

He pushes his way through lines of people. The crowds are piling up in the concourse for the second time today and the sounds of voices and clattering luggage echo up into the roof of the terminal. Just as he reaches the door by the reception desk a hand pulls at his arm.

'Excuse me, what time is the ferry to Roscoff?' An old man in a grey suit stands behind him, sweat dripping on his worried face.

'Just queue over there. They'll be boarding in half an hour.'

'Oh, thank you. My daughter. She's meeting me there,' he wheezes as he bends to pick up his suitcase.

Steve closes the door and starts to run up the stairs. Then he stops. Fuck. The Roscoff boat left at eleven. That's the Santander ferry they're queuing for. Never mind, he says as he sets off again, it's not my problem now, is it? No, it is his problem. He goes back down and searches through the crowds until he finds him.

It's another hour before he gets to Elise's office. He stops to catch his breath, straightens his tie and pulls back his shoulders. Ready, he thinks, just be calm. Clear and calm. The door is slightly open and he's about to knock when he hears a low groan and a snuffling noise from inside. He pushes slowly and looks into the room. A pair of shoes pokes out from behind a desk near the wall. Cherry red Doc Martens. Steve recognises them straight away. He tiptoes forward and leans over to see Andy on his knees with his head on the chair, pressing his face into the soft fabric.

A small cough from the doorway makes them both jump. Andy scrambles to his feet and pins Steve against the wall as he rushes past and stands to attention at his side.

'Now,' says Elise. 'Which of you boys wanted to see me?'

*

'I hear you're leaving,' Rachel says, as she sips at her milky coffee.

Steve puts his brimming cup of lemon down on one of the staffroom chairs and sucks his scalded fingers. 'Yes, I saw Elise yesterday. She wasn't happy.'

'I'm not surprised. There'll be no one left soon.'

'She made me promise to clear all the queries first.'

'That'll take ages.'

'No, I did them this morning'

'All of them?'

'Yep, I rang everyone and told them there'd been a computer failure. Cancelled them all.'

'What computer?'

'Exactly. But none of them could argue.' Steve shrugs. 'So I'm done. The list of lies is in the bin. Elise is moving Andy to the gîtes desk so he'll have to make up his own.'

'What's he being punished for?' she smiles.

'For being Andy. That's enough, isn't it?'

Rachel turns away and looks out of the window. 'Dylan's asked me to go and see a film with him at the arts centre.'

'God! Not Eraserhead?'

'No, Annie Hall.'

'Ah, that's OK. You'll like it.'

'I know. I've seen it twice before. I haven't told him that, though.'

She takes a piece of paper out of her pocket. 'Here's my address if you want to keep in touch. What are you going to do now anyway? University, like you said?'

'Oh, I don't know,' Steve says. 'I was thinking about buying a van and going to Ireland.'

He checks his desk again, opens all the drawers and throws the final scraps of paper into the bin. As he reaches for his bag the internal phone rings.

'Steve, there's someone at reception asking for you.'

'But I don't do reception.'

'He asked for you specifically. Said his name's Saltram.'

He looks over the partition. 'Dylan, how would you like to meet someone from the House of Lords. He's downstairs. Tell him I drowned in the harbour.'

He picks up his bag, taps Dylan's shoulder as he walks past, then sprints along the corridor and down the stairs two at a time. Pushing through the fire exit to the car park, he walks quickly round the back of the portacabins towards the sea. In the fresh air he starts to slow and relax as the warm sun spreads a smile across his face. He looks out over the dock for the last time. The ferry in the distance has left its usual rippling wake across the water, but something else is churning beneath, breaking the surface into peaks and deep hollows. When he's close to the landing jetty a black mass crashes up from the depths and lunges over the dockside with sheets of water falling away from its shining hulk. A cavernous eye, dark and empty, stares at him as its tentacles writhe in the air, flinging thick black slime over the stone walkway.

He stops, looks back over his shoulder, then runs forward with his arms outstretched, laughing.

'Come on, you fucker!' he shouts. 'I've been waiting for you. Come on, then! Come on!'

The Japanese Library

I had only been working in the college for a few days and people were already asking me, 'What are you going to do about the Japanese Library?'

I was surprised. There was no mention of a Japanese Library in the job description and nobody had said anything about it in my interview. But I was the new head librarian and everyone assumed it was my responsibility. A few colleagues smiled as they told me that it was a 'health and safety nightmare', but apart from that I didn't know what problem I was expected to solve.

For the first week or two I went around the college, getting to know the campus and meeting people in other departments. The Japanese Library was mentioned a few times, but it was only when I spoke to the Estates Manager that I understood why it was causing so much concern. She told me it was in the basement of a building that was due to be demolished to clear a site for a new lecture theatre. The offices and classrooms would be relocated, but no one knew what to do with the Library.

'What about the department of Japanese Studies?' I asked.

'There is no department of Japanese Studies,' she said.

I walked over to the building she had pointed out, which was already being emptied. Rubbish skips and old furniture filled the loading bay in the yard. I found my way to the rear staircase and went down into the basement which appeared to be deserted. All I could see were bare concrete floors and two rows of identical grey doors. Heating pipes ran along the ceiling and machinery hummed from a boiler room nearby. I walked to the end of a dimly-lit corridor and saw a sign on a small piece of card that said 'Japanese Library'.

There was no answer when I knocked, so I opened the door slowly and entered the room. It was impossible to tell how large it was at first as I couldn't see farther than a few feet in any direction. The space was completely filled with bookshelves closely stacked in long rows. Walking to the end of the first row I found a route into another aisle, then another. I felt I was entering a labyrinth and all I could do was follow the trail to see where it led. The shelves were full of books and loose copies of magazines. The top of each row was stacked to the ceiling with more books, and piles of journals eight feet high stood against the walls, almost blocking the way. It all looked very precarious, as though a shove or even a rush of air could topple everything over.

I heard a cough and a shuffling sound in the distance, and as I turned the corner of another set of shelves the top of a man's head appeared behind a pile of boxes.

'I heard you,' he said. 'I heard you coming.'

'Hello. Has anyone ever talked to you about health and safety? This is a nightmare.'

'Yes,' he said, 'I've heard that too.'

He stood up from his chair. He was a tall man, at least six feet three, with dark hair and a close-cut grey beard. He looked like an old academic in his tweed jacket and knitted tie, but he was so broad that he filled the little space that was left in the room and I felt small in his presence.

I introduced myself as the new college librarian, and he said, 'This is the Japanese Library, so I suppose that makes me a librarian as well.'

Although I didn't say so at the time, I wasn't convinced. This doesn't look like a library to me, I thought, this is just a hoard, a landfill of paper.

'This is the main room,' he said, 'but there are four more just along the way. I'll show you.'

He led me back between the shelves and out into the corridor. He opened the doors to the other rooms and I could see they were as densely packed as the first.

'I have been building this library for over twenty years, and it is now the largest collection of Japanese scientific literature in the country.'

'Is it all catalogued?' I asked.

He answered me sharply, 'I know where everything is. If anyone wants something I can find it.'

We walked back to the first room and he stood looking at me, belligerently, his eyes never leaving my face.

'How often is the collection used,' I asked, 'if there is no department of Japanese Studies? Do science researchers come here?'

He was still staring. 'You have a job to do down here, don't you?'

'Yes,' I said, 'I do.'

He looked down and his shoulders fell as he opened the door to his room and went back inside.

*

After my visit to the basement I spent a lot of time thinking about the Japanese Library. I borrowed keys from the Security Office and looked around the rooms late in the evening when the building was empty. I thought of making a basic inventory to understand what I was dealing with, but soon gave up on that task. I couldn't find any structure or order at all, and most of the books didn't have any content in English. I tried to estimate the amount of material, but apart from the crowded shelves and piles of journals there were boxes that hadn't even been opened. Every time I went there, more boxes had been delivered and stacked higher in any available space. Every time I left I felt defeated.

I was so preoccupied with what I had found that I neglected my other work. The staff in the college library were probably surprised that they saw so little of me, as I kept myself out of sight and out of their way. The truth was that I was unable to concentrate on anything else and was becoming more and more lethargic. I spent my evenings in the Japanese Library, wandering between the rooms, picking up indecipherable books and discarding them again, trying to count the journals then abandoning the numbers when they became meaningless. More than once I found myself pushing against a long row of shelves, making it sway from side to side, then stopping the movement with my hand before everything came crashing down.

*

One morning as I sat in my office, with the door closed as usual, I found a hand-written letter in my mail.

Dear sir,
When we met recently I said I understand that you have a task to carry out here. Before you do, I think I should tell you something about the Japanese Library and how it came to be the collection it is today. I know you have been visiting the Library at night, but I doubt that you have found anything that will have told you its story, or indeed mine.
I first came to this college almost thirty years ago to teach English to overseas students. I have no other language skills, and you might be surprised to know that I do not speak Japanese. The little that I am able to read I picked up myself from the books that have passed through my hands. In those early days there were fewer foreign students and the classes were small. They were mostly

scientists and engineers from Germany and Italy, but there
were also some from Korea and Japan. In one of my classes
there was a young Japanese student who was very clever
and very keen to learn. In fact he was one of the best
students I ever taught, and he was the only one I ever came
to regard as a friend.

He was here to study metallurgy and to learn English,
but he was also very interested in history. He used to ask
me questions about our industrial heritage which was
something of an interest of mine. One Saturday as I was
walking near the Tanfield railway I saw him waiting for
the steam train that was run by volunteers on the old line.
Seeing how interested he was in the locomotive, I offered to
take him to the Railway Museum in York and we went there
together the following weekend. This was an unusual thing
for me to do, and it was not something I felt I could tell my
colleagues. Looking back, I think that I was a little ashamed
of our arrangement, but we had a very fine day together. I
can see now that it was one of the happiest days of my life.

The summer term ended a few weeks later and my
Japanese friend graduated with a Masters degree. As I
expected, he had the best results in his year. He planned to
travel in Europe before studying for a doctorate in
Germany, and he asked if I could look after his small
collection of Japanese books until he could arrange for
them to be collected. Of course I was happy to do so. When
he left he said he hoped that he could return one day to

teach at our college and encourage more Japanese students to study here.

Over the following months I received a few parcels from him. They contained books in Japanese that he had picked up on his travels and I kept them with those he had left with me. I thought I would try to add to his collection and I wrote to some publishers in Japan to ask if they would make donations to what I described as our Japanese Library. I must admit I was surprised when boxes of books and journals started arriving, so I wrote to other publishers and more boxes followed. Before long I ran out of space in my small office and I asked a caretaker if he knew of somewhere I could store them. He showed me a room in the basement and lent me a set of keys so I could move them there.

I never got around to returning the keys, and by the time the caretaker retired a while later I had taken possession of the room. I managed to acquire some old bookshelves and the Japanese Library started to become a reality. As time went by I moved into the other empty rooms in the basement as well, and now you have seen the result of my work. Although I haven't heard from my Japanese friend for many years, the boxes keep arriving and I try to find room for everything I receive. As I have been here for so long I am rarely disturbed. Occasionally an official looking person will find their way to the Library and ask a few questions, but they never return. Recently there was a new Safety Manager who was troublesome for *a while but then he stopped visiting as well. Since I gave up teaching fifteen years ago to devote my time to the Library, I have seen fewer familiar faces. But I have always been here, waiting for a knock on the door, each time hoping that my friend will walk in and see what I have created for him.*

As the years have passed it has become harder for me to keep up with the amount of work I need to do, and I know that I am running out of both space and time. I have almost given up hope that he will return. But now you are here, and I can see you have something to accomplish for your own peace of mind. All I can say is that I will not hinder you. I am not happy to see you, but I am content with what you have to do.

*

The day after I received the letter I contacted a disposal company and arranged for them to clear the basement of its contents. My only concern was that no one else in the college should find out what I was planning to do. Academics can be very sentimental about books, regardless of their subject matter, and even if they have never seen them. If any of the lecturers found out that the Japanese Library was about to disappear – that its entire contents would be reduced to pulp – there would have been an uproar. I could already imagine their letters to the college Principal, and angry articles in the academic press.

The trucks arrived late at night and were hidden from view at the rear of the building. The Japanese Library was removed shelf by shelf, box by box, and room by room until the entire basement had been emptied. The whole operation took five nights to complete and each night I was there to supervise the work, making sure that not a single book or journal was left behind. The workers from the disposal company were very thorough. After they had removed every scrap of paper, they swept out the basement and cleaned each set of shelves from top to bottom.

On the fifth night, after the last truck had left, I took the sign off the door that I had entered just a few weeks before. I walked through the rooms, and in each of them all I could see were rows of clean and empty shelves. Nothing was misplaced, everything was in order and everything made sense. I realised that I had, for the first time, created my perfect library.

The Longhouse

Cam led me along the walkway between the wooden buildings of the longhouse. The sun shone directly overhead and the bamboo planks burned through the thin soles of my shoes. I followed close behind him and watched the sweat seep from his hairline and run down the back of his neck, darkening the collar of his shirt. When we passed an open door he clapped his hands at a yellow shape lying under the porch step.

'Ha!' he said, 'Even the dogs look for shade on a day like this.'

Everyone else in the group had gone whitewater rafting, but as I had asked Cam a lot of questions about himself and his family he offered to show me his home. I wanted to spend more time with him so I was happy to stay behind. As we walked along he pointed to a single-storey building which stood further away among the trees, surrounded by forest ferns and shrubs.

'An English man lives there,' he said. 'He married a woman from our village and built that house for her.'

'What does he do here?'

'He is very old. His wife died a long time ago and we take care of him. He is part of our family now.'

At the end of the longhouse we stopped outside a small windowless building. Cam ducked under the low doorway and stepped into the gloom. I followed him inside and blinked at shards of daylight that pushed through gaps between the walls and the roof. He stood with his back to me, muttering rhythmically under his breath. The room seemed to be empty but as I walked past him I saw a small metal cage suspended from a beam at the same height as his head. His hands were raised, palms upwards, and he was staring at the white face of a human skull behind the bars.

When he finished speaking he took a key from his pocket and unlocked a door at the side of the cage. He took the skull and held it out in front of him, looking at it closely from all sides.

'I had to apologise for disturbing him. To show respect.'

'Who is it?'

'I don't know for sure. One of our ancestors, I think – or maybe an enemy from an old battle,' he said with a smile. 'We are Christians now and pray in church. But it is important that we keep our traditions.'

Cam rolled the skull gently around in his hands. He looked very still and calm, as though he was thinking of things far away from his work as a tourist guide, driving a minibus and learning languages at night school.

'Is there just the one?'

'There were others, but they were stolen. That is why we keep him in this cage. We look after him and he protects the longhouse.'

The skull glowed in the darkness of the room as Cam caressed it, and I wanted to hold it in my own hands, to feel the smooth surface of the bone. I wanted to wrap my fingers around him and touch the cool depth of his thoughts. To press my thumbs into the hollows of his eyes and see the forest paths he had walked, and the waterfalls and pools where he dived and swam. I wanted the sharp edge of his jaw to draw blood across my palm.

'Can I hold him?'

'No,' he said, 'You don't know the words.'

'You can teach me the words, Cam.'

'No. Only the shaman can teach the words. And he has not been here for years.'

Cam put the skull in its cage and turned the key, and we went back outside into the blaze of the afternoon. My polo shirt and chinos were damp with sweat and my shoes were beginning to blister my heels. I looked over to the house in the trees and saw an old man in a white vest sitting in the shade of his verandah. He raised his hand and I waved back.

I wonder if he knows the words, I thought. I wonder how long you have to stay here before you can learn the words.

Aniela and James: a love story

If I hadn't gone to Hexham I would never have met James but this story begins, as so many love stories end, with a simple mistake. I caught a train there because I had applied for a job at a home for old people. I already worked at night in a hotel in Newcastle and I needed to earn extra money to pay for a university course that was starting in the autumn. But I never went for the interview. The journey took longer than I expected and when I saw the home I turned around and walked away. It reminded me too much of the buildings where I grew up, with its rough grey concrete walls and blank windows.

The town had nothing else to show me, just a few quiet shops and cafes, so I followed the signs to the abbey which I could see rising in the distance behind the market square. As I walked through its narrow doorway the sound of the organ reverberated around the columns and high into the roof. Bach, I thought. Yes, it could only be Bach. There were about fifty people inside, most of them in the first four rows so I went to sit near the back with a few others. On the far side of the aisle I noticed a man had spread a handkerchief on his lap. He took something from his pocket and unwrapped it, a slice of pale cake, and he ate it slowly, one small piece at a time. His eyes were closed and the light from one of the tall windows shone down on him. He was smiling to himself. Are you allowed to eat in church, I wondered, here in England? Without a priest to bless the host?

When the music finished we both walked towards the rear door and I made sure we reached it at the same time. He stepped to one side, shuffling awkwardly with a parcel he was carrying. There was a small crumb of cake at the corner of his mouth, and a few more on the front of his jacket.

'That was lovely, wasn't it?' I said.

He looked puzzled as he picked the crumb off his lip.

'The music, I mean. I love Bach, don't you?'

'Yes, yes, it was very good,' he mumbled.

He shifted his parcel from one arm to the other. It looked like he might drop it and I reached forward to help.

'It's alright, it's not heavy. Just some books I picked up earlier.' He nodded over towards the square.

'Is there a bookshop? I must have missed it.'

'It's a small place but I buy a few things there. Old illustrated books mostly.'

He started to move away so I asked quickly, 'You like art as well?'

'Ah, these are by Heath Robinson. So I suppose it is art,' he smiled. 'And strange contraptions.'

I had never heard of Heath Robinson, and as I walked along beside him he started telling me about his drawings of impossible inventions. It all sounded very English to me and quite childish. But while he was speaking I could see that he was older than I first thought. His face was unlined but there were broken veins on his cheeks and his hair was grey and swept back in a style no one else had worn for a long time, even in my country.

He was still talking about Heath Robinson and his books when he stopped next to a car and took out some keys.

'Is this your car? It's beautiful,' I said as I bent down and looked through the window. Inside it was like a drawing room in an old house with deep red leather seats and dark wood.

'It's a Daimler. My favourite,' he grinned.

'I've never been in a car like this before.'

I stood with my hand on the door and waited for him to say something. He hesitated for a moment. 'Would you like a lift then? But I'm not sure where you're going?'

'I was going to catch a train back to Newcastle.'

'I live in Newcastle as well. In Jesmond. I'll take you if you like... If you don't mind.'

'Oh, that would be great. My name's Aniela, by the way.'

He raised an eyebrow.

'It's a Polish name.'

I held out my hand but he stepped back and pretended to touch the brim of a hat.

'James. At your service.'

As I got into the car I thought this might be a lucky day after all. But there's a saying, isn't there, that luck doesn't make itself?

*

James made a show of driving very carefully. He sat upright in his seat, both hands on the steering wheel, looking straight ahead. It was warm in the car so I took off my shoes, but he still had his jacket on over a thick cardigan. He smelled slightly almondy, like marzipan, and I wondered what else he was carrying in his bulging pockets.

He didn't seem to want to talk while he was driving, so I told him why I had been in Hexham that day, about the job and the interview I didn't go to. He just nodded and said, 'Mm, I see.'

Then I told him more of my story – how I had come to England to study for a masters in psychology, and that I was working to raise the money for the fees. I told him about my home and the city I had left.

'Ah, Wroclaw.' he said, 'Previously known as Breslau, of course. And Vratislav as well, when it was part of Hungary, but that was a long time ago.'

'You seem to know a lot about my home.'

'I know a lot about history, I suppose. My mother says I live in the past. And she's from Hungary, so I pick these things up along the way.'

We were both quiet for a while and when we reached Newcastle I asked James if he could leave me near the university. I didn't want him to see the shabby house where I rented a room. He stopped in the road behind the library and walked around to open my door. When I got out he seemed nervous, rubbing his hands together and looking down at the ground.

'My mother's quite old now,' he said, 'and I think she could do with some help at home. She says she doesn't, but I know she struggles sometimes. If you don't mind working with old people, maybe you could come and help her. If you think it would suit you. And we'd pay you of course.'

'Well, yes, I'm used to old people. I looked after my grandmother for a long time.'

I wasn't sure what to say next, I didn't want to seem too keen. 'So what shall we do?'

'Why don't you come and meet her first? To see if she likes you. And to see if you like her as well. She can be a bit bossy but she's a good sort really.'

*

Two days later I went to the address James had given me. I had walked in that part of Jesmond before and seen the big houses and gardens. It looked like a fine place to live, much better than I could ever hope for. I followed the numbers until I reached a house with three cars in the drive, the Daimler and two old sports cars, all polished and shining in the sun. James must have been looking out for me and he waved from the porch.

'Aniela, I'm so glad you came. Come in and meet mother.'

He closed the door behind me and led the way down the hall.

'She's in the kitchen as usual,' he said.

I could smell onions and paprika cooking, and as I followed him into a room at the back of the house I saw a small, white haired woman sitting at a table cutting up a piece of meat. The knife shook slightly in her hand.

'Mother, this is Aniela.'

'Ah, you must be James' new friend,' she said. 'It's nice that he brought you to see me.'

'Er, yes. I met James in Hexham the other day.'

'He told me. In the abbey.' She pressed her lips together in a thin smile. 'He also said that you might be able to help me. I'm not sure I need any help, but he thinks I do.'

'I'm happy to do anything I can. Anything you'd like me to.'

'And you're from Poland, he said. You speak very good English.'

'Thank you. I've been studying English for a long time. And French and German. I know some Hungarian too.'

'Tényleg beszél magyarul?'

'Igen. Egész jól beszélek. I worked in a restaurant in Budapest for a year. I learned a lot there.' I was relieved that she used some of the few words of Hungarian I knew.

'Wonderful! James, that's wonderful! She can help me cook. Do you know how to make lecsó and goulash soup?'

'I think so.'

'Good. My name is Ibolya, but you can call me Ibbie. And I'll call you Annie. That's only fair, isn't it? I think we will get on very well together, Annie.'

I glanced over at James who was standing by the kitchen door, looking very pleased with himself.

*

We agreed that I would go to the house for a few hours on three days every week. That suited me as it wasn't far from where I lived and I would still have time to spend in the library, preparing for the course. My job at the hotel reception had long hours, but it was quiet once the guests had all checked in and then I could find some time to read. Weekends were the worst, dealing with drunk people all night, but I found I could manage them if I stayed calm and didn't let them think I was their friend.

James' mother was happy to have someone to talk to and help her with the cooking. She really only needed me to prepare the meat and vegetables, stir her cake mixes and clean the pots and pans – all the heavier work that she found difficult herself. I was relieved that she didn't expect me to cook lecsó as my few months in Budapest were spent taking orders and washing dishes. Although I knew what goulash looked like I wouldn't have known what to put into it.

On my second visit, while I was peeling potatoes at the sink, she said, 'I have looked you up Annie. I know more about you than you think.'

I must have looked worried because she laughed and said, 'Just your name – Aniela. It means Angel, doesn't it? It means you are kind and merciful.'

'It's a common name in Poland. But, yes, it comes from the word for Angel. And your name means Violet, the flower.'

'You know that! Yes, it does, but I don't like the English word. It's an old person's name. Do you know how old I am, Annie?'

I didn't, but she told me. She also told me how she had come to England in 1956 after escaping from Hungary with her parents when there were tanks in the street outside their home. She was only eighteen when she met her husband soon after they arrived, and then married him a year later.

'He was a good man, Annie, and a good husband. But I don't think he was ever a good father to James.'

'Why do you say that?'

'James was always a disappointment to him. My husband was very successful in his work and he expected James to do the same. But he was a quiet boy. He did well at school, but not well enough for his father. He did give him a job later, though, copying and filing in one of his offices. James said he did all the easy work, and he did it for a long time.'

'But he doesn't work there now?'

'No. When his father died, they said they didn't need him anymore. He wasn't sorry to leave. But my husband had made

76

sure we were comfortable. We have this house, and we have enough money for James to spend on his cars and his books.'

'There seem to be a lot of books.'

'Yes, probably too many. But there is something else about James – he's fifty-eight years old and I don't think he has ever had a girlfriend. None that I know about anyway.'

'Doesn't he like women?' I asked.

'Oh, I think so. He certainly doesn't like men, if that's what you mean!'

She stood with her head on one side, looking at me.

'You have a pretty face, Annie. And nice hair.' Then she looked down to my hips, thighs and ankles. 'But none of us are perfect, are we?'

*

Ibbie often asked me to stay and eat with them after we had cooked. I was happy to, as the food was so good. We prepared goulash, of course, and I learned how to make lecsó with peppers, tomatoes and paprika. We made hortobágyi pancakes, potato dumplings and spicy fisherman's soup. Sometimes she would complain about the ingredients, saying that the peppers weren't as sweet as the long yellow peppers she remembered from when she was young, and that the paprika from Waitrose was never red enough. So I bought bags of paprika for her from a Polish shop I knew and the food tasted even better than before. Every day the kitchen was filled with the smell of baking and stew simmering on the stove. James loved to eat. His favourite dish was chicken paprikash, served in a deep white bowl with crusty bread. His face would disappear into the bowl for a long time, and when he sat up with the thick red sauce dripping down his chin he looked like the happiest man in the world.

He would usually disappear to his study after we had finished eating. It was my job to clear the table and wash the dishes. I didn't mind. I was getting paid, after all.

One day Ibbie asked me, 'Has James shown you his library – all the books in his study?'

'No, he hasn't,' I said. 'He tells me about the new ones he has bought sometimes, but I haven't seen them all.'

'Take a look when he's not here. That will be better than asking him. Look at the books hidden at the back of the high shelf behind his chair. I wonder what you'll think.'

*

James was out when I was next at the house, so as soon as I had finished in the kitchen I went to find his study. I had never been upstairs before and I was surprised at how shabby it looked beyond the main hall. Everything was clean, but there were bare patches on the stair carpet and the wallpaper was scuffed at the corners. It looked like a place where people had grown old together and never felt the need to change.

The study was a small room at the front of the house and from its window I could see James' cars. He must have liked to be able to look at them from where he sat. As well as a desk there were two chairs – a deep leather armchair and an old office chair – and the walls were lined with shelves. I expected to find a computer in the room, but I remembered that James said once that he didn't want a computer at home because he would just find too many books to buy. He preferred the booksellers' catalogues that arrived every week in the post.

I looked along the shelves at the rows of books on history, old buildings, transport, all the things that he was interested in. Then I reached up to the top shelf and moved some of them out of the way. I could see others lined up behind, as Ibbie had told me. They were ordinary looking books with titles like *The Salon*, *The Drawing Room* and *In the Boudoir*. I lifted a few down and opened them to find page after page of old black and white photographs, all of women in their underwear or partly undressed.

As I looked through them I thought they were strangely touching, these pictures of women with shy smiles and awkward poses. Most were young but very few of them were thin. How fashions in bodies have changed, I thought, as well as in clothes. I took more of the books down and I could see they were antique collectors' editions of some sort. A few of them showed pictures of naked women, but even they seemed coy and rather sweet, with their bottoms in the air and their hands covering themselves. I could imagine James looking at them with the same smile I saw when he ate cake in the abbey.

*

Whenever James wasn't at home I went back to the study to look at his hidden collection. I enjoyed turning the pages slowly to see the photographs of those lovely innocent women, caught long ago in someone else's gaze. I thought of them as innocent because they were so still and timeless. Nothing could touch them in that moment and nothing would now. I felt very close to them as I sat in the study, quiet and alone. After a few visits, though, I guessed that James knew that I had seen his books because the ones with the naked pictures disappeared and the space was filled with others. But I didn't look for them. They were far less interesting to me than the women in corsets and stockings who I felt I recognised and knew.

The next time we all ate together, James was very quiet and he left the table as soon as we finished our soup. Ibbie went to her room to rest and after I had washed the dishes I walked upstairs to the study. I knocked lightly on the door. There was no answer but I knew he was there, so I turned the handle and stepped inside. He was sitting in his armchair with his eyes closed and a book on his lap. I could see that it was one of his collections of photographs. I sat down in the chair opposite him.

'James.'

He didn't answer but I could tell he wasn't sleeping.

'James, what are you looking at?'

He moved his lips slightly, hesitating, then said, 'It's a room. A large room with heavy curtains and pictures on the wall. There's a thick rug, a small table, and a chair.'

'Who is in the chair?'

'It's a young woman. She's facing a mirror but I can see her eyes, she's looking at me.'

'Tell me what she looks like, what she's wearing.'

'She's wearing...' He stopped for a moment. 'She's wearing a corset and, um, suspenders and stockings and her hair is dark and pushed up high on her head. Yes, and a pearl necklace. She's smiling. She's very beautiful.'

'Open your eyes, James. Look at me. What do you see now?'

'The same,' he said. 'Just the same.'

I stood up and left the room quietly, and went to fetch my things from the kitchen. As I walked back through the hallway James came downstairs and stood by the front door, red-faced and anxious.

'My mother doesn't know about my books. But I can't give you any more money, Aniela. I'm sorry, I just can't.'

'James,' I said, 'I don't want anything from you.'

He handed me a small package. 'Please, take this. I'd like you to have it.'

As I took it from him I could see that it was a book wrapped in tissue paper. I opened it in the street, once I had walked far enough away from the house not to be seen. On the cover was the title *Peter and Wendy* and the name of the author, J.M. Barrie. I knew about the boy Peter Pan. I had seen him in a film I loved when I was a child.

*

I wasn't sure what to do with the book which was old and possibly valuable. I really did need to save money and thought I would try to sell it, but I had no idea where to go. Then I remembered the bookshop that James had mentioned when I first met him. On my next free day I caught the train to Hexham again and walked up to the town and through the market square. Past the gift shops and charity shops, tucked in an alley behind the main street, I saw the sign *AB Books – Anthony Black, Antiquarian Bookseller*. It was a very small place with hardly enough room to walk around between the shelves and display tables. A man sat at a desk facing the door and he looked up as I entered. He was younger than I expected, wearing jeans and a leather jacket. I probably looked surprised. I had assumed that only old men were interested in old books but he was much closer to my own age.

'Hello, can I help you?' he said.

I reached into my bag and took out the book.

'I'd like to sell this, please, if you are interested.'

He unwrapped it, turned it over, and opened the cover.

'Where did you get this?' he asked, looking at me closely.

'A friend gave it to me. It was a gift.'

'A friend?'

'Yes, a friend.' I held his gaze. I was determined not to look away.

He started flicking through the pages of the book, glancing back at me as he did so. Then a slip of paper fell out onto the desk in front of him. We both read the writing at the same time:

To Aniela, with heartfelt thanks
James

He closed the book and put it down on the desk between us.

'I can give you a hundred and twenty pounds. If you have ID and proof of your address.'

'Yes,' I said, 'I always have my documents with me.'

*

When I went to see James again in his study I asked him the same questions that I had before, and he told me what he saw. He sat in his armchair with his eyes closed and described a bedroom and a large four-poster bed draped with heavy red fabrics. There were gold-framed pictures on the wall and a nightstand with a white bowl and pitcher. At the foot of the bed stood a chaise longue, with a woman lying across it in a green silk negligee. That was his word – negligee.

'James,' I said, 'this picture is all in colour.'

'I am colouring it by hand, like an old photograph,' he smiled.

Before I left the room he gave me another book. He held it out to me without saying a word.

Over the next few weeks we continued to meet after I had completed my work downstairs. I sat opposite him and prompted him with questions: 'What is she doing, James? What's she wearing? What does she look like?'

And he told me what he saw, his imaginings. I don't want to call them fantasies because I knew they came from the photographs he had been looking at. Once or twice I thought I even recognised the scene and the woman he described. Then he gave me a book and a few days later I would take it to Hexham. My exchanges with the bookseller were always short – he took the book from me, told me a price and I accepted. The amount he offered went down slightly each time, but I knew I wasn't in a position to bargain with him.

*

I still cooked with Ibbie on my regular days. She taught me how to make Hungarian desserts and pastries and the poppyseed cake that James liked so much. I brought hazelnut puree from the Polish shop and we made Gundel pancakes together, filled with the sweet nutty paste and covered in melted chocolate.

One day I offered to make pierogi and borscht, to show her the little that I knew from home, and she was delighted.

'Peasant food!' she said, 'James will love that.'

She was quiet as she watched me press out the dough and make up the little parcels with potato and cheese.

Then she said, 'Annie, when you talk to James in his room does he ever touch you?'

'No,' I said, 'never...'

'I didn't think he would. But does he ever touch himself?'

'No, I'm sure not.' I felt myself blushing bright red.

'Good. His father always told him to be careful of himself.'

After I had made the borscht I went upstairs. James was sitting in his armchair, waiting for me. I sat in my usual place and he described for me a kitchen in a large house, with bowls and plates spread across a wooden table and a fire blazing in the hearth. A woman kneaded dough on a board with her apron falling open and the tops of her breasts uncovered.

'Is she beautiful, James?'

'Yes, her face is flushed, her eyes are shining.'

'This doesn't sound like one of your photographs.'

He didn't reply.

'Do you want to touch her, James?'

He rubbed his hand on the arm of his chair. His mouth opened a little but no words came. A tear fell slowly onto his cheek. I stood and leaned over and I kissed him – not his cheek, just the tear. I kissed it away.

*

Near the hotel where I worked there was a signboard at the side of a road that I walked past every day. It advertised a store called *Pulse and Cocktails* with a picture of a woman wearing a maid's outfit and holding a feather duster. She pouted at the camera, or rather at everyone who passed by. I had never been in a sex shop before but the picture of the young maid intrigued me. So I looked up the address and found it near Scotswood Road, between a carpet warehouse and a garage that repaired motorcycles. It didn't seem like the kind of place anyone would normally walk to.

The store was bright with fluorescent lights and shiny surfaces. Behind a counter a man wearing a *Pulse* tee-shirt was unpacking boxes. He said something over his shoulder and a young woman came out from a back room and walked over to me. She looked as though she was dressed for a night out with her short skirt and strapless top. Her hair was long and blonde and her fingernails very pink. She must have thought I was nervous and smiled cheerfully at me.

'Hi. What can we do for you then?'

'My, er... boyfriend,' I said. 'He likes old-fashioned clothes, underwear, things like that.'

'You're looking for some lingerie?'

'Yes. I'd like to buy something to wear for him.'

'What sort of look, do you think? Slutty, cheeky?'

'I don't know. Something nice.'

She looked at me, up and down. 'I think I know what you mean. Let's have a look over here.'

I followed her over to a rack on the far wall, where she lifted down two plastic packets.

'These are corset and stocking sets, with suspenders. The black one would suit you.'

The picture on the front showed a woman sitting in a cane chair with her legs crossed and her finger on her lips as though she were saying shush.

'We don't accept returns, but this one should fit you. Yes, you're about the same size as me. And it's only thirty pounds.'

I looked at her, and looked down at myself. Am I really like her? The same size, the same shape, the same sort of person? Yes, I suppose I am, I thought, or I could be.

We went back to the counter where I paid and folded the packet into my bag. As I carried it home it felt so light that I hardly knew it was there. It felt like nothing.

*

Next morning I put on the corset and stockings. I also found a tiny pair of panties in with them. I had never worn anything like this before and when I looked in the mirror I thought I looked stupid. A stupid girl whose thighs were too fat and white, and whose knickers were too small. But the corset hugged me closely and I liked that, even though the material was cheap and thin. I put on a little make-up and a necklace of fake pearls and pinned my hair up at the back. Then I stepped into a light summer dress, put on my usual sensible shoes and walked out into the street.

By the time I reached the house I felt hot and uncomfortable with the corset clinging to my skin. The late summer sun was burning my arms and the back of my neck and I was glad to go back indoors. Ibbie let me in and waved towards the stairs.

'I'm looking for a recipe, Annie,' she said. 'Do you want to go and see James? You know where to find him.'

I didn't knock on the study door. I opened it and walked straight in. James sat where I expected to see him, with his eyes closed, smiling slightly as he always did.

'Hello, Aniela. I heard you at the front door.'

I stepped forward, put down my bag, and undid the buttons on the front of my dress. I let it fall to the floor and sat down opposite him with my legs crossed.

'James. I don't want to listen to you today.'

'What...what's wrong?' he said.

'I just want you to look at me.'

He did as he was told. I knew he would. But when he opened his eyes, when he saw me, his face which was usually so smooth and boyish creased and crumpled like old paper.

'No,' he cried. 'No, that's not right. That's not what I meant.' He got up and rushed past me and I could hear him running down the hall.

I stood up and put my dress back on. I let my hair down and took off my necklace. As I looked around for one last time – I knew it would be the last time – the room where we had talked so often seemed very small. There were just shelves, a desk and two chairs. And the books, of course. So many of them. A bag lay on the desk with yet another old book inside and I wondered what his latest enthusiasm might be. I took it out and turned it over. It was a copy of *The Wind in the Willows*, the same one I had taken to Hexham the week before. I recognised the small blue ink stain on the cover. The bookseller had taken a few pounds off for that. I looked around the shelves at all the first editions and illustrated books. There were no gaps. Every copy that James had given to me was in its place. He must have gone to see Anthony Black every week and bought each one of them back.

When I went downstairs Ibbie was waiting for me.

'Aniela, I don't think you should come here again. James is very upset. I know you meant well – at least I hope you meant well. But no more, please.'

I just nodded. There was nothing I could say.

'He asked me to give you this.' She handed me a large envelope and walked back to the kitchen.

*

I left the house and walked from Jesmond towards the city centre, through Brandling Park, past the university and onto Northumberland Street. The September sun was still shining and the pavements and shops were crowded at that time of day. With my headphones on and the Brandenburg Concertos playing on my iPod I felt disconnected from it all. The summer was coming to an end, my summer with James, but I had saved enough money to pay for the course that would start in a few weeks' time. I could stop working in the hotel, I'd study, make new friends and plan for the future. It was all I came to this city to do.

At the railway station I sat on a bench and waited for the train to Hexham, counting the number of times I had made the journey over the past four months. I knew every stop along the way now, and every rattling bend through the Tyne Valley.

I wondered if I would ever go there again. Maybe for a concert in the abbey? Probably not. I picked out the envelope Ibbie had given me and opened it. The book was old, as I expected, with the title embossed on the cover: *My Line of Life* by William Heath Robinson. I flicked through the pages of comic drawings and elaborate inventions but there were no slips of paper hidden inside this time. Instead I found a dedication written in ink:

To Anniela, with love
James

I closed the book, kissed it gently, and put it back in my bag.

Jeannie's Clock

I was out on the front blasting the drive with my power washer when a car pulled up over the road. Oh dear, this looks like trouble, I said to myself, old Len won't be happy. Everyone knows he hates people coming to his house these days. Those Jehovah's Witnesses got a right bollocking when they knocked, and even Elaine was shocked at the way he carried on.

A man got out of the car, looking smart enough with his suit and briefcase, but I was still surprised when Len opened the front door and they shook hands. We had hardly seen him for weeks. Even when I went over to ask if there was anything we could do – like you feel you have to after a funeral – he didn't answer.

Maybe it's an estate agent, I thought, when they went inside. He might be going to move now he's on his own. I shouted to Elaine and we waited by the window until Len's visitor came out again. It didn't take long, there was another quick shake of the hand and he was away.

'Is that Jeannie's clock he's carrying?' she said. 'The one she took to the Antiques Roadshow?'

'Looks like it. You don't think he's sold it, do you?'

'I hope not. She loved that clock. Her mum left it to her.'

'It was quite valuable, though. That expert on the programme said it was worth a few thousand.'

'All the same. Why would he do a thing like that?'

*

A couple of days later I was on my way back from the shops with a newspaper and two more strangers were coming out of Len's house. They were carrying a table and I watched as they loaded it into the back of a van. Inside I could see four dining chairs and the old glass cabinet that Jeannie kept her ornaments in. A man with keys on his belt had a big grin on his face.

'You want to get in there,' he said. 'There's loads of stuff going.'

'What do you mean?'

'It's all on Gumtree. Have a look. Seems like he's clearing out.'

When I got inside I opened my laptop and searched Gumtree for anything in our area. I soon found a long list of things with a local phone number in Furniture and Household Goods. Three-piece suite, Dressing table, Sideboard, and so on, with *No reasonable offer refused* on all of them.

Within an hour there were more people at the door. When they were leaving I walked over, as casual as I could, and caught Len on his porch.

'What's going on, Len? Are you moving?'

'Just having a bit of a clear out.'

'Is everything OK?' I said, tapping the wallet in my back pocket.

'Oh, no,' he said, 'nothing like that. Just things I don't need any more.'

'I'll take your car off your hands, if you like. I've always fancied that one.'

It was a lovely car too. A Jaguar XF, top of the range. He always looked after it and polished it every Sunday. I asked him once how he kept the alloys so clean and he waved a bottle with an expensive looking label at me.

'That's my car,' he said. 'Nothing to do with her. It's not going anywhere.' He started to go back indoors, then hesitated. 'There is something you could do, though. If Elaine's still helping at the charity shop, could she take some of Jeannie's clothes in?'

*

Elaine went across the road and came staggering back with three full bin liners. Then she went over for more.

'I thought he was going to ask me to help sort Jeannie's things out,' she said, 'but he'd already bagged them up. You ought to see in there. The place is almost empty. There's nothing left in the living room, just a camping chair in front of the telly.'

'Well, there must be something left. He's carrying more out now.'

Len had set up a pasting table at the edge of his lawn and was piling stuff on top of it. From our window I could see plates, bowls, cups and saucers and more things from the kitchen – a breadmaker, food mixer, coffee percolator and other odds and ends. He put up a hand-written sign that said *Please help yourself.* An hour later it was almost empty. I went and had a poke around but all I managed to pick up was an old toaster and a blue teapot with a cracked lid. By the end of the afternoon someone had taken the table as well and there were just a few things left on the grass.

When it started to get dark I saw Len back outside. He was looking down at the lawn, pushing the last bits of crockery around with his foot. He bent down and picked up a broken saucer, then dropped it again. Then he stood with his hands in his pockets, looking back at the big blank face of his house. Elaine gave me a shove so I went over and tapped his arm.

'Here, Len. Do you want this?' I said, holding out the teapot.

He turned and looked at it. I didn't know if he recognised it at first. His eyes were thick and damp.

'Oh. Aye, thanks,' he said. 'Yes, I could do with a brew.'

'I'll bring a cup over if you'll make me one as well.'

*

At the end of the week Elaine came home from the hospice shop and said, 'You'll never guess what. Len came in today and asked if we still had Jeannie's clothes. We hadn't started sorting them yet. They were still in the stockroom in bags, so he took them all away again. He gave us fifty pounds and I told him he didn't need to, but he insisted.'

Next thing I heard from a neighbour that he had seen him doing the rounds of the second-hand shops in town. I think he must have been looking for the furniture he had sold on Gumtree, at least the pieces the local dealers had picked up. The white transits started appearing at his house again, dropping things off now instead of taking them away. I saw the table and dining chairs going back in, and matey with the keys was grinning more than ever. Then a big new sofa arrived in a Barker and Stonehouse van. It looked just the same as the one he had sold. Boxes were delivered from John Lewis and Argos and I hoped there was a new teapot in there somewhere, because he definitely needed one.

As the weather got better I saw Len more often, cleaning his car on Sundays again and even putting some new plants under his kitchen window. I wandered over, just to be sociable.

'You look busy, Len.'

'I thought I'd have a clematis here,' he said. 'Jeannie always liked them.'

'That's nice. It'll get the sun there. Speaking of the sun, are you thinking of getting away anywhere this year?'

'No, that was her thing. I don't need a holiday. I'm alright at home.'

As I turned to go back across the road he said, 'Pete, I've just thought, have you still got a video recorder? Mine went out with all those other things. I've found a tape of Jeannie on the Antiques Roadshow with that old clock of hers. I'd like to take a look at it again if I could.'

The Life and Sulphurous Death of Theo D

Theo as a boy: Hamburg, 1947

Großmutter:

I never liked the boy. He was stupid and he was dirty. He always smelled of sour milk and piss. I could never wash it off him. We would never have taken him if he wasn't the son of our son, the one who didn't come back from the war. Then his mother disappeared and we felt there was no choice. I always said she was a whore from the docks and so she proved when she left. Probably with a sailor from one of the foreign ships. He was a clumsy boy and he broke things. He didn't know how to hold a spoon properly, or a cup. He couldn't sit straight or look you in the eye. Even when I scolded him, which was often, as I had to, he stared at the floor or at his shoes smiling to himself. And he was dirty. He used to piss in the yard in corners, leaving his wet marks on the wall.

Großvater:

It is true that his Oma did not love him but Theo was a good boy. It's also true that he stained the walls, but what man doesn't enjoy the freedom to piss on a wall from time to time? He was his father's son and that was enough for me. On Sundays I would put my hat on his head and take him walking. We walked along the U-Bahn and I showed him the sections that I was rebuilding – the tracks on the streets, the underground stations, the tunnels. We saw some of the old carriages that had been burned out in the firestorms. I taught him the names of all the stations, and even though he couldn't read he would remember them and recite them in order. Theo was not good with words, but I taught him how to count and how to measure correctly, and I taught him how we laid tracks one rail after another. We would stop at a bakery on Wagnerstrasse to buy bread. Then I took him to meet my friends in the bierkeller where we sang songs about hunting in the old times, and I'd say:

'Here is Theo! When he is grown he will work with us on the railway. One day he will be a great engineer!'

***

Theo's disgrace: Hamburg 1962

The passenger:
Of course I remember Theo. Everyone who used the U-Bahn in those days knew him, or rather they would have seen him and maybe spoken to him. He worked in the newspaper kiosk in the underground station at Wagnerstrasse. No matter how early your journey to work, or how late the last train home, he was always there wearing a black hat with a feather, the kind old men used to wear. The old line on the U-Bahn was very poorly kept at that time. Some of the trains had been running since the railway was built over fifty years before. The stations were dirty and full of litter, but Theo's kiosk was clean and tidy. He kept his newspapers and books in order and the tobacco and cigarettes were always stacked up neatly.

One thing that puzzled me about Theo was that I don't think he could read, or if he could read he could not read well. I watched him one day as he stared at an advertisement for automobiles on the arch opposite his kiosk. He was mouthing the sounds Bcc Em Vcy over and over, as though he was trying to fix them in his mind or force them to mean something. But he knew the names of all the stations, and all the streets and districts on the lines. If anyone asked him for directions he answered quickly and with great confidence. He must have learned them and gathered them in his head like a map. You might wonder, though, how he managed to sell newspapers and books if he couldn't read the titles, but his regular customers knew they had to point at what they wanted. Others would get annoyed and shout at him. Theo looked terrified until he understood what they were after. I am afraid that some people would torment him by asking for something and then standing to watch the panic grow in his face. I probably did that myself once or twice; I am not proud of that.

But Astrid was always kind to him. She was a young photographer who lived in my apartment block. She was beautiful, and moved with the ease and grace that only young people have. She always carried a camera and she watched the world all the time looking for the shape and gesture she wanted to capture. She was one of the few people who talked to Theo, and she might have photographed him as well. I guess he looked interesting in an odd way. I like to think that he can still be found in one of her pictures, maybe in a book or an archive. He will never be seen here again, that's for sure.

Astrid had a companion at that time, a young English man named Stuart. She said he was a painter and that one day he would be a famous artist. He was a handsome boy, and they were such a fine-looking couple. I heard that he was also a musician who played with a rock and roll group in the bars and cellars. Needless to say that meant nothing to me, but I know that Astrid spent a lot of time with them all. Stuart used to talk to Theo when he bought his cigarettes from him, though I can't imagine what they spoke about as they had little language in common. But I remember seeing them together and Theo was saying 'Ja, ja' and Stuart was echoing him 'Yeah, yeah... yeah', laughing at themselves and each other.

I mentioned that Theo kept his kiosk and his part of the station very clean. He was always gathering scraps of paper and litter from the floor and tidying them away. One day I noticed that when he picked up used matchsticks he put them straight into his jacket pocket. It was such an odd thing, and after I had seen him do this a few times I asked him why he wanted them. He looked at me as though this was a very interesting question and said, 'I am building a model railway. These are for making wooden carriages, but I need very many of them. Do you know how many carriages there are on the Hamburg U-Bahn?' I assumed Theo was going to tell me, but he leaned closer and whispered, 'I don't know yet. I am still counting.'

After that I came into the habit of saving my matches for Theo. After I lit a cigarette, I put the spent match back into the box and when the box was used up I left it on the counter of his kiosk as I was passing. I didn't stop and talk, as I knew he would start on a long description of the U-Bahn – which stations were built first, which was the biggest, or the busiest, and his latest calculation of the number of carriages. Besides, by this time Theo had started to develop a strange odour on himself or on his clothes. He always appeared clean, but he began to smell quite sulphurous. He had the taint of scorched matchwood and old fire about him. Other passengers and passers-by must have noticed as well, but I suspect I was the only one who knew the reason.

It was a few months later, in April of that year, when I heard of the disaster at Wagnerstrasse. The station was closed as I was going to work and I had to walk to the new line at Wartenau instead. On the train people were talking about a fire on the old underground platform. They said it had started at the newspaper kiosk and I immediately thought of Theo. It took no more than a day before people were blaming him, saying that he always looked a strange type and that they never trusted him. Rumours always fly quickly when nobody has any facts. At first they thought that he had died in the fire, but no body or remains were found. Some stupid people said that he always smelled like a devil and that he had jumped into a tunnel when the flames started, back to where he belonged. I also heard that he was seen running from the station, heading down Hamburger Strasse towards the harbour.

Nobody saw Theo again but he had certainly left his mark. There was a black stain from the fire on the platform that was not cleaned for months. There was a scorched calendar on the wall whose date was never changed again. It showed 10 April 1962. Later I realised that was the day that Stuart died.

***

Theo in exile: Liverpool, 1965

The landlady:
I don't know why he came here, and he wasn't able to explain. He could hardly speak any English when he arrived. There

was something about a train, something about a boat, and something about a man called Stu. I've no idea who that was because he didn't seem to have any friends. It was hard to talk to him. If he didn't understand what you were saying he would say 'Yeah, yeah, yeah' and laugh to himself. This was the kind of thing that got him into trouble – that and his funny hat. More than once he came in the worse for wear after someone had battered him in the street. His German accent didn't help.

He started doing a night shift in a bakery, and he'd come home in the morning with bread and cakes that he'd share. We hardly saw him really. I think he spent a lot of time at Lime Street watching the trains. I saw him there once or twice when I was going to Chester to visit my sister. He always looked very lonely. Then he worked in a hospital as a cleaner. There was no bread anymore, but he brought home these horrible smells instead. You knew when he had come in the front door and walked up the stairs, even without hearing him. When he left, his room was clean and tidy but I had to leave the window open for days. He said he was going to Crewe, something to do with trains. The last thing he said to me was, 'Did you know that eighty-seven trains are at Crewe every day?' Well I didn't. Who would know a thing like that?

The ticket inspector:
Theo? That funny German one? He was always at the station. Always asking questions. Where has that train come from? Where is that train going? I didn't really know what he wanted. I'd point him at the information board, but that didn't

seem to help. Mostly he sat watching the trains, eating bread from his pocket, counting the carriages. There were a lot of spotters in those days. Mostly boys with notebooks writing down the engine numbers. You could pay a penny for a platform ticket then. I said to him once 'Why don't you go and ask them? They know all the trains.' 'No,' he said, 'They do not understand the railway, and they do not know how to count correctly.' It was a pity, really. They might have talked to him. Nobody else would.

***

Theo's good heart: Haltwhistle, 1978

The cafe owner:
Haltwhistle is the exact centre of the country. Did you know that? Theo told me that if you cut out a map and hang it up and draw a straight line top to bottom, then do it again from two different places, the centre is where the lines cross. Isn't that clever? He came into my cafe one day and when I asked him what brought him here, he said, 'I wanted to see what it was like where the lines crossed.' He never said very much, so that was quite like poetry for him.

No one knew where he had come from, but he stayed around and set himself up in an empty bothy on the edge of the forest. He threw a tarp over the broken roof and tied it down and that was where he lived. He wasn't bothering anyone so people let him be, except for some small boys who threw stones at him and called him names. He never did anything about it so I shooed them away most of the time.

He used to come in for a cup of tea now and then, but he only ever had a few coppers on him. He was very thin and looked all scooped out in the middle, so one day I had an idea and asked if he would wash some pots to pay for the tea and a cake. Well, he was at them straight away and did such a good job I got him to come back again. Soon he was cleaning for me every day, just for an hour or so, and I could tell he knew his way around with a mop and bucket. I couldn't afford to pay him much but I always sent him away with some leftover scones or a sandwich.

Considering how he lived, he kept himself tidy enough. He smelled like a clod of earth and pine needles most of the time, but I didn't mind that. There are worse smells in the world. He must have been growing vegetables – potatoes and carrots and the like – near the bothy, because he started bringing them in for me as a present. One day he brought some flowers he had picked and gave them to me. 'Oh, Theo,' I said, 'I'm old enough to be your mother!' And he smiled the sweetest smile, but there was a dampness in his eyes as well. The only time we fell out was once when we were in the little kitchen together and he leaned in as though he was going to kiss me. I gave him a stern look and he left very quickly that day.

Mostly he was a quiet one, but he got very excited once. He had heard about the new Metro they were building in Newcastle, and came in shouting, 'They are going to have a U-

Bahn!'. I didn't know what he meant until he told me about his grandad's railway when he was a boy. After that he would catch a train into the city now and then to watch them digging the tunnels and laying the tracks. That was when he was happiest, I think.

Then one day he just scarpered. He got into some trouble with the forestry workers and they came looking for him in the cafe one morning. They said he had been scraping the red paint off the trees they had marked for cutting down. When Theo came in later I asked him what he had done, and he said, 'They shouldn't be destroying things. Trees, living things, or anything!' I told him that was their job, but he wouldn't have it. That was the only time I ever saw him angry. And as it turned out that was the last time I ever saw him at all.

When I came in the next day there was a small bag of potatoes by the door, but no sign of Theo. Later I walked down to the wood and I could see the tarp on the bothy had been on fire and smoke was coming out of the roof. I'm not sure if the men from the forestry burned him out or if he did it himself. I don't suppose it really matters now either way.

I never expected to hear about him again, but one day my neighbour Winnie came back from Newcastle and said she had seen Theo on one of the new Metro trains. She didn't recognise him at first because he was dressed in neat clothes and was wearing a black hat with a feather. He was riding up front near the driver, looking like a lord, she said, like he owned the train. I was so pleased. He had a good heart really, and deserved to make better of himself.

***

Theo in tears: Newcastle upon Tyne, 1990

The gallery attendant:

I was working as a volunteer at the Side Gallery at the time. It was a great place, run by people who really cared about photography, and we held a lot of exhibitions, by new photographers as well as some of the big names. It was a very social place too. People used to come in to see the pictures and videos, or to use the library, and sometimes just to sit and talk. You would get to meet all sorts and that's one of the reasons I liked it so much.

After I had been there for about six months, a German chap started coming in. He was always dressed a bit oddly and looked like an old hippy with his embroidered waistcoat and his hat and his long curly hair. We got talking and he told me his name was Theo. I could tell he was a photographer because he always had that vinegary smell about him that you get from a stop bath. He said he had a darkroom at home and he developed his own black and white prints. He was keen to show them to me and said he would bring some in. When he did it was a suitcase full, and every single picture was of a railway or a train. A lot of them were details of trains: wheels, windows, seats, doors, luggage racks, everything. He told me proudly, 'I have 3,216 pictures of the Newcastle Metro. Next week I will bring in some more.'

It turns out he had a job on the Metro, but not as a driver or anything technical. He worked every night in the depots cleaning the graffiti off the trains. He'd been doing it for ten years. I didn't even know that was a job, but it's all Theo did, every night.

Anyway, we had an exhibition coming up by the German photographer Astrid Kirchherr, the one who lived in Hamburg at the same time as The Beatles. She had taken a lot of the early pictures of them. Theo had mentioned that he was from Hamburg and I thought he was about the right age to have been in the city then. I was looking forward to seeing him to ask him if he was there at the time. I wondered if he might even have seen them.

I went into the gallery on the day the exhibition opened and the other attendant, Lucy, said 'Your friend Theo's upstairs.' I went up to the main room on the first floor and I could see him walking along looking quickly at each photograph, in a real hurry. Then he stopped in front of one picture and stood staring at it for a long time. He was so focused on it that I didn't want to disturb him, so I waited a while and then walked up behind him. It was a portrait of Stuart Sutcliffe, the one who died. I said 'Hey, Theo,' and when he turned around to look at me, I could see his face was wet with tears.

***

Theo redeemed: County Durham, 2015

The neighbour:

The first time we saw Theo he was pushing his heavy old bicycle up the path towards us. We knew it was him, it couldn't have been anyone else. We had been told about his odd clothes – his short green jacket and matching trousers that ended just below his knees, the long socks and patent shoes. But we hadn't expected the size of the feather in his hat or the hunting horn slung over his shoulder on a leather strap.

When my wife and I moved into the small estate in the Derwent Valley several people had said, 'Have you met Theo yet? You will soon enough. But be careful, if you talk to him you'll never get away.' We soon found out that this was true. Theo liked to talk, but only about one thing. 'Hello,' he said, 'Did you know this used to be a railway line? I have a model railway in my house. I made it myself, all with my own hands. Would you like to see it?'

Of course we made the mistake of talking to Theo. Everyone did. It was hard not to when he set his bicycle in the middle of the path and waited when he saw you coming. You couldn't easily pass by without exchanging a few words. 'Hello. Did you know there was a railway line here until 1966, and fourteen trains took coal from the mines down to the river every day. I have a model railway in my house...'

To try and avoid the topic of trains and railways, I once asked Theo why he always pushed his bicycle up the long path towards Consett instead of riding it. His answer was very simple, 'I am only 60 kilograms!' As he leaned towards us I could see that he was thinner and older than I first thought, and when he took his hat off there was a stripe of white in the middle of his dyed black hair. A chemical smell came from his clothes, like glue and paint thinner, and he was off again: 'Did you know I have a model railway? It's all made by hand.'

We started avoiding Theo and took care to check that he wasn't coming in either direction before we set out on a walk. But there was always a chance that he would appear around a bend in the path or that we would see the unmistakable shape of his hat and feather coming towards us in the distance. I became more terse and abrupt each time we met, refusing to do more than nod in passing. One day he called out as we walked away, 'I am very lonely, you know!' Of course I knew, but I couldn't carry the weight of his loneliness in my conscience.

I saw Theo for the last time when I was out walking by myself one day. I stepped down onto the path from the old railway bridge where he stood underneath the arch, peeing against a wall. He looked more ragged than before, with stains on his jacket and scuffed shoes. He heard my footsteps and looked back at me as he turned and buttoned his fly. He grinned like a small boy caught in mischief then picked up his bicycle and wheeled it away.

After a few weeks we realised that Theo hadn't appeared for a while and I asked a neighbour if he had seen him. He said he hadn't, but told me that he had put a video on YouTube, something to do with his model railway. I would find it easily, apparently, just by searching for his name. I couldn't resist looking for it. Although Theo talked about his railway all the time, I had never been tempted to ask him about it, much less to go and see it. But I was intrigued that he would do something like that.

The video was easy to find. There aren't many Theo D...s on YouTube. The title appeared – *The Hamburg U-Bahn: a real model, all hand made* – under a shaky image of a station platform. The picture was gloomy with low resolution, but I could see people wearing clothes from the fifties or sixties sitting on a bench and waiting at the platform edge. Pieces of litter lay strewn in corners and wet grime marked the tunnel wall, staining a poster that advertised BMW. The gravel between the tracks was dark with spilled oil and dirt. After a long wait, a light emerged from a tunnel and an old red and white U-Bahn train came silently towards the platform and stopped. Nothing stirred, every figure stayed fixed in its place. Then the train started again and moved away.

This sequence repeated twice more before the camera drew in closer to show a newspaper kiosk piled up with tiny papers and books near a staircase to another level. As it moved past the kiosk and up the steps, a long street came into view with buses, cars, shops and larger buildings. More underground stations could be seen in cut-away sections beneath the pavements, with trains moving around the tracks above and below the road, stopping, starting and stopping again.

Gradually the shot pulled back and the miniature vehicles became smaller, the streets narrowed, and even the tallest buildings shrank away. The city stretched out toward the edges of the screen and grey harbour walls rose up in the distance. The sea shone at the periphery of my vision and I felt I could reach out to touch mountains and clouds.

Then, suddenly, the edge of a table appeared with the back of a chair leaning against it. The camera moved up to survey the room, taking in the whole of the model city which filled it from wall to wall. There were some pieces of heavy furniture in the background and paintings hanging from a rail – landscapes and hunting scenes. Everything in the room looked dark and old. As the image continued to rotate, a mirror appeared on the opposite wall and Theo came slowly into view with a small camera held in front of him. He caught sight of himself and stopped with a look of panic on his face, as though he had seen a stranger looking back at him. He dropped out of sight below the edge of the table and the picture jumped sharply, becoming dark and unfocused.

Nothing happened for several seconds, and I could see from the timer on the screen that the video was coming to the end. But then slowly the camera moved upwards again, creeping over the table top, up over the railway track and the platform, above the small figures with their luggage and the passing red and white trains. It tracked up to the street, over cars, buildings and the city until it reached the wall and the mirror where Theo stood smiling, with his arm extended over all that he had made.

***

Theo's apology: here, today

I apologise for nothing.
For being born, for the life I lived,
and, in all probability, for the death I will die.

I do not apologise for carrying the odours of the world with
me.
When I worked on trains, I smelled of the railway.
When I worked in the bakery, I smelled of yeast.
When I cleaned the hospital, it was shit and death.
These things absorbed into my skin and clothes.
It was not my choice.

There are some things I regret.
I am sorry that I did not kiss Astrid
and I am sorry that I did not kiss Stu.
They were my only friends.
Nobody touched me and I have touched nobody
since I held my Opa's hand sixty years ago.

I do not apologise for leaving my stains,
or for the things I destroyed.
I have spent my whole life cleaning and rebuilding.

Did you know there are 374 carriages on the Hamburg U-Bahn?

One day the flame of a single match
will take them all again.
The trains, the stations and the city.

Along with my sulphurous self.

And I make no apology for that.

Intensive Care: small stories

Rabbits

When I was a small boy, four or five years old, rabbits lived at the end of my bed. Every night they ran to and fro beneath the covers. I could never see or touch them but they always kept me awake, hopping around in the dark.

Then they went to live under the bed and became creatures with long arms and hands. I kept my feet tucked away so they wouldn't grab my ankles and pull me down.

Eventually they moved to the attic, with all the other ghosts and monsters. One day my father found me standing rigid at the door to my bedroom, staring up at the black space where the hatch had blown aside.

'What are you afraid of, you daft bugger?' he said, 'It was only the wind.'

*

Now I'm sitting with a haematology consultant at the Freeman Hospital.

'We have the results of the biopsy,' he says, 'and I'm afraid you have myelodysplasia, with monosomy seven.'

'I've never heard of that. What is it?'

'Rabbits,' he says, 'You've got rabbits in your bed. You must have noticed them. They've probably been keeping you awake at night.'

'Yes, I'm tired all the time. I've had no energy to do anything for months. That's why I'm here.'

'Well, without treatment they'll move under the bed and grow arms and hands. Then they'll catch you and pull you down in the night. The only option is a transplant – if that's successful we'll get them into the attic and keep them there.'

'But what if it isn't successful? What if the hatch slips? If it opens?'

The doctor looks down and sighs. 'Yes, well,' he says, 'that will be the wind.'

Wednesday Morning

Eight thirty, Wednesday morning, and the day is beginning in the usual way. You sit on the toilet with the lid down, pressing your forehead against the cold edge of the washbasin. Head throbbing, bile in your throat, wondering if you might vomit and whether it will help when you do. Christ almighty, you think, I've done it again.

Too many beers last night, and then the last of the weekend vodka which you necked from the bottle in the garage when your wife was upstairs. You promised you wouldn't. Promised yourself, that is, not her. But you do that every day, believing you mean it.

You stand and look in the mirror. Your face is red, your eyes redder, and the pus-filled lumps around your nose are getting worse. You breathe into your hand and sniff. Too late to do anything about it now. You're almost beyond caring if anyone notices as you walk back through the office to your desk, but you keep a tissue in front of your face just the same.

Two meetings in the diary, at nine and eleven. Luckily you're only in the chair for the second so you can sit back and say nothing for the first. If anyone looks your way you'll push a few papers around and tap at your laptop so it looks like you're taking notes.

By eleven your head is clearing, and you know you'll be OK. All you have to do is keep the next meeting brief and defer a few decisions. The serious work can wait 'til the afternoon. You'll get a sandwich for lunch, walk round the block, shake your aching bones out, avoid the chatter. You might even look at some travel websites, book a weekend away. God knows she deserves it, putting up with you, ignoring the way you carry on. Maybe Prague or Krakow. Beer cities. You remember the hotel in Warsaw with sparkling wine and vodka on the breakfast buffet. You didn't see much of the place that day. Or the next.

Turning back to your screen, you shake your head. You'll make it better, try harder. You won't have so many beers tonight. Maybe just one or two. Not quite sure how you'll get through the evening otherwise. You could stop at the corner shop for a few cans of Stella on the way home. Just a four-pack. Pint cans, of course, not the small ones. They're much better value when you work it out.

Stanley

The vicar hurls round the corner at the end of the road, black and spidery on his old bike. We stand and watch as he props it against the wall and rushes into the flats, up the stairs, two at a time.

'He must be going to see Stanley's mum,' David says.

Little Stanley lived with his mum on the third floor. She had taken him to the beach with his cousins and he never came home. All we heard was that Stanley went off by himself and disappeared, washed up later on the shore. I can see him curled in a rockpool with his eyes closed, tiny crabs scurrying around, red sea anemones opening and closing as the tide washes over. He must have been in shorts and tee shirt because that was all I had ever seen him wear. I can't imagine him in swimming trunks.

We know it's sad but the truth is none of us liked Stanley much. I'm not even sure of his real name. We called him Stanley because he was very small and wore little round specs.

He might have joined in with football in the car park once or twice when we were short of players but no one wanted him in their team. Usually he played with the girls. They treated him like a kid, but he didn't seem to mind.

Once in the woods a couple of older boys grabbed him and pulled his shorts down. Filled his pants with dead leaves and pulled them up tight. He waddled away crying, like a baby with a full nappy. I thought it was mean but that was all.

At the end of the week, the vicar's back, waiting outside the flats until two black cars arrive. A line of people come down the stairs behind a man with a white coffin in his arms. I know Stanley must be inside but it looks too small, like a box for a doll.

'Is that his dad?' someone says.

'Don't think he had a dad.'

When the cars leave we start playing football again, but our heart isn't in it. Just a few kicks up and down. Nobody tries to score a goal. We stand by the railings looking up at the flats. I try to work out which one Stanley lived in. One of the windows is probably his bedroom.

'What time is it? I'll probably go home and watch telly.'

'I dunno. Four o'clock?'

'Stanley had a watch,' Kevin says.

'Stanley?'

'Yeah, it was a bit crap. He said his mum gave it to him for his birthday.'

'He couldn't even tell the time.'

And there's Stanley in the rockpool, with his arm stretched out in the water and his little white-faced watch shining in the sun.

Training Partner

You look out of the window, but there's not much of a view. A small patch of grass, a footpath that stretches around the back of the hospital, the gardens of a few houses.

Every evening a woman runs around the path, circling the building. She leans forward when she runs and you think of the words *Progressive acceleration*.

In here people come and go at a steady pace. They all wear masks, aprons and surgical gloves. You can hear them through the door as they prepare themselves in the outer room – the tearing of the plastic aprons from the roll on the wall, the snap of the gloves on their wrists. Some of them leave after a few minutes and you want them to stay longer. Some linger and you want them to leave.

The woman eases her pace as she runs by, then accelerates again. Today must be *Interval training*. You know she can't see you. The windows are tinted so there's no view in. People shouldn't look into cancer wards. They might not like what they see.

The nights are the same as the days, but with fewer visitors. That doesn't mean you get to rest. The magnesium drip is set up at midnight, but you're woken for observations at 2, awake again when the bag needs replacing, a cup of tea at 4, more observations. You drag the drip stand to the bathroom, then drag it back. Pills, breakfast, the day begins again.

Sometimes she runs by in the morning as well, but not every day. *Recovery time.*

At 7 someone comes to take your glass and water jug away. 'Back in a few minutes', she says, but you know it will be at least an hour before they're replaced. So every morning you fill your glass and hide it, then pretend to be asleep when she comes in. She looks around, tuts, then leaves. It's your small win for the day.

The runner walks a short distance, checks her watch, looks towards the building then sets off again. *Mile Repeats.*

There's an exercise bike in the room. To help regain your strength, they said. One turn of the pedals today, maybe two tomorrow. Then three and four. There's no hurry. The days will become weeks, and time will pass.

The woman runs into view, stops, looks up at your window and waves. You wave back. She's training for a big race, and you've been picked for the endurance event.

07:30 Newcastle to London

He always thinks the day's going to go well when he gets a table to himself in the quiet coach with plenty of room to spread his things around. So Paul put his coat on the luggage rack, his briefcase on the seat beside him, and took out his notebook, phone and laptop. He had three hours through to London to get some work done, with maybe a bit of breakfast after York. But when the train stopped in Darlington someone came through the door behind him, dropped a bag by the window and sat down opposite. He carried on looking at his screen, and just caught sight of a thin blue jacket, shabby and long in the sleeve.

The man didn't say anything and Paul wasn't going to. There's no point talking to strangers at that time in the morning. He caught his leg with his foot once and said sorry, that was all. But when Paul glanced up he was looking back at him, just vacant, not much there really. He knew straight away who he was.

'Alec,' he said. 'Alec Silcock. I'm right, aren't I?'

The man focused, looked again, but there was still no response.

'It's Paul. Paul Walsh. We were at school together. At Abbey Comp. What was it? Fifteen, seventeen years ago?'

'Yeah. Yeah, you're right. Paul. I remember.'

Paul held out his hand. Alec kept his right arm under the table, put out his left hand and tapped the back of Paul's with his knuckles. His fingers were yellow and dirty under the nails.

'It's been a long time. But I was sure it was you.'

Yes, it was something he saw in his eyes and mouth, even though Alec's smile looked sour now when he spoke.

'I wouldn't have recognised you,' Alec said, looking him up and down.

'Well, I've put on a bit. Good living, I suppose.'

'Yeah, I suppose.'

'How about you? You joined the air force, didn't you?'

'The army. Engineers. I finished my time.'

'Where have you been? Where were you posted, like?'

'Here and there. Never in one place long.'

'Iraq? Afghanistan?'

'Like I said, just here and there... And you?'

'I got into construction and trained as a QS,' Paul said. 'I'm a project manager now in the Newcastle office.'

'Yeah, I thought you might end up as a manager. With your notebooks and your pens.'

Alec tried to pull down the zip on his jacket with his left hand, but it stuck part way. Still tugging at the tab, he brought his right arm up and pressed it against his chest to hold the zip, but when Paul looked at his sleeve he quickly put it back under the table. He squinted at him then looked away.

'So how about family? Have you got any children?' Paul asked.

'Yeah, two boys. Eight and ten. They live with their mother back in Manchester. Good boys, though.'

'Your little soldiers, eh?'

'No. They're better than that.'

He started pulling at his zip again then gave up, looking down the carriage, back over his shoulder.

'Do you remember we used to sit at the back in Geography?' Paul said. 'Throwing darts at that target on the floor. Old Taffy never knew where the noise was coming from.'

'No. I don't remember that.'

'Go on, you must do. Me, you and Martin Vaughan at the back of the class.'

'No, I don't.'

'You remember Martin though?'

'Yeah, I gave him a hammering once for taking the piss.'

Just then Alec stood up and walked to the end of the carriage and out of the door. A minute later the inspector appeared and Paul showed him his ticket.

'Someone else here?' he asked, looking at the dirty holdall on the other seat.

'No, that's mine.'

After the inspector had worked his way down the carriage, Alec reappeared and sat down again. He looked out of the window. There didn't seem to be anything more to say, so Paul tapped a few keys on his laptop and tutted a bit, trying to look busy. It wasn't long until York so he started putting his things away, and took his coat down from the rack.

'Well, this is me. It was good to see you, Alec. Take care.'

'Yeah, you too.'

But he wasn't looking at Paul. He was looking at the reservation card on the back of his seat. 07:30 Newcastle – London.

Martello Tower

I should have known it was time to go home when I was knocked over by a security van outside Trinity College. It hit me square on my right side and threw me across the road. A few people ran over and helped me to my feet. Someone fetched my glasses from the gutter. Luckily they weren't broken, just bent and scratched, like the rest of me. I staggered away muttering, 'Thank you. I'm OK. Really. I'm OK.'

I must have been stunned because I went into the nearest shop, bought a postcard and scribbled: 'Gabrielle, you won't believe what just happened to me...' Then I remembered that she had dumped me, and that was why I had been travelling around Ireland on my own, on the trip we should have made together. I was there to prove something to myself, or to her. I tore up the postcard and threw it away.

The whole journey had been wrong from the start, when I was taken away for questioning by Special Branch at the ferry port in Fishguard. It was 1981, at the height of the hunger strikes, and I must have been conspicuous as a young man travelling to Ireland alone – with a name like Connolly.

It didn't get any better. I wandered the streets of Cork for three days without speaking to anyone. I arrived in Galway during races week and everywhere was full. Eventually I found a room that I had to share with a god-bothered American who spent a long time telling me where I had gone wrong with my life.

Then I got badly sunburned walking from Gort to Coole Park, where I sat amongst the reeds on the edge of the lake hoping to see Yeats' wild swans. In Limerick I was bitten by fleas in a cinema as I watched *Clash of the Titans* – a desperate choice just to keep out of the rain.

On a cross-country train my bag fell from the luggage rack onto a group of men who were playing cards. Their money and drinks flew everywhere. I was shoved over and called an eejit.

So by the time I reached Dublin I was already battered and raw. Then the security van hit me. It was my last day and I had saved the highlight of the trip to the end: a visit to Sandymount to climb the stair of the Martello Tower. I limped to a bus stop at Townsend Street, just missed one and waited half an hour for the next. We got as far as Irishtown when the bus broke down. It was a lost cause. I was lost. I crossed the road and caught the next bus back to the city.

At eight o'clock that evening I staggered onto the Liverpool ferry, with a lump on my head and a bruise the size of Ireland and as black as a pint of Guinness blooming on my right thigh.

Gabrielle, I thought, I made it on my own and it was fine. Everything was fine.

A Hat

Maybe he'll buy a hat. A wide-brimmed white hat with a black band to wear with a silk and linen suit. Then he can sit on a terrace in the sun drinking cold beer as he did in Phnom Penh, watching the pimps and dealers going about their business in the street below. Or the Stetson he tried on in a store in Austin where the owner laughed and said he'd never be a cowboy. Perhaps a kufi from Marrakesh, a Basque beret, or the tweed flat cap that will turn him, finally, into his father.

He pulls at his scalp and drops loose clumps of hair into the sink. A razor sits on the bathroom shelf with a can of shaving foam. Whichever hat he wears to cover his baldness, he knows he will never travel again.

He first fell in Røros, then collapsed again in Riga. In Sitges he sat on a hill overlooking the bay and wept because he knew it was the last time he would see the town. Now he's in a small room and the only trip he can make, the one that drains all his energy, is the long shuffling walk to the toilet. The foreign accents he hears are those of doctors on their rounds and the nurses who bring him medicines and food. He never asks where they are from because he is the stranger here, a guest in this antiseptic place.

He dries his head and studies himself in the mirror – the long jaw, protruding ears, his father's nose. And his pale, bare scalp. The best thing about losing all your body hair to chemotherapy, he has been told, is that it takes much less time to dry yourself after a shower. It's good to know that every hard journey has its compensations.

Robin's Day

On Friday morning Robin came down on the 6.30, with a window seat and breakfast on a tray. The train was almost on time. He walked out of King's Cross station, around the square and turned right onto Euston Road. As he passed the St Pancras Hotel he could see the shape of a man on the pavement ahead of him, laid out between a lamp post and the kerb. In a glance he saw his dark hair, his grey coat, black shoes and a Waitrose carrier bag still in his hand. It looked as though there were papers in the bag, or folders. It was hard to tell so quickly.

Robin hurried on, worried that he might be late for his meeting. And nobody else stopped, he would say to himself later. From the moment he first saw the man on the pavement to the point where he passed him, nine people walked by. Maybe more. Robin lost count at nine.

By the time he reached the British Library he was sweating and breathing heavily, but the calm bustle inside the building relaxed him. He stood near the entrance waiting for his ID badge, recognising colleagues, nodding hellos. Caroline came up to him.

'Robin, how are you? How are things in Newcastle?' she said.

'I've just seen a man collapsed outside, near the hotel.'

'Oh, no. That's awful. But there are always paramedics by the station. Have you seen them on their bikes? That's such a good idea with the roads so busy... It's good to see you again.'

They were escorted to the conference room. Robin always looked forward to these meetings. He liked the surroundings and the care they had taken with the building. Even in the staff areas they had wood panelling on the walls and door handles bound in brass and leather. They know how to look after themselves down there, he told everyone back at home.

At coffee, he was juggling a Danish pastry on a napkin when he found himself standing next to Phil from Leeds.

'Phil,' he said, 'did you see that man on the pavement near King's Cross as you came in? I think he might have been dead.'

'He was probably drunk, or drugged up. It's always like that around there. Anyway, have you heard about our ebook project? You might want to do something like that. It's an expensive business, though...'

The meeting followed its usual course. Robin was well practised by now, volunteering for the easy actions early on the agenda. Then he was off the hook later when the serious work was discussed, if he could get away with it, which he usually did.

Tom was at lunch. He didn't get down from Aberdeen very often these days and Robin was pleased to see him. He was good company, always ready with a joke and a story.

'Tom, I saw a dead man today. Out on the pavement.'

'Really? I had to deal with a body once on Iona, on one of our summers there. It was a young lass, washed up on the beach in a terrible state. It took three of us to wrap her decently and take her up to the cottages. The police said we should have left her until they came, but she'd have been washed out again. Poor wee thing, she was.'

*

At the end of the afternoon, Robin left for his train while the others stood talking. He was in a hurry to get the five o'clock as he had a seat booked in first class. Expenses wouldn't cover it all, but he didn't mind paying a bit extra from his own pocket to get a meal and a couple of drinks on the way home. And he knew that if he smiled at the women with the trolley they were usually quite free with the bottle on a Friday.

By the time they reached Newark he was on his third glass of red, filled to the brim. He'd had enough of emails for the week, and he sat back in the rattle and sway of the train. London was a long way behind and it was only another two hours to home.

As he looked beyond his reflection at the darkness outside, he saw himself on a quiet road he had never walked along before, a row of terraced houses, early evening with the streetlights coming on. He watched two policemen open a gate and walk up the path towards a door. No, one was a man and the other a policewoman. They knocked and shuffled their feet, looking at the ground. The door was opened by a woman, smiling, then not smiling when she saw them. A young girl held on to her leg with a thumb in her mouth, half-hiding behind her. On the stair in the hallway was a boy, slightly older, looking puzzled. The policewoman was saying something to her. The woman raised her hand to her mouth. The policewoman reached out and touched her elbow, gently. Then she handed her a Waitrose bag. Which she dropped to the floor. And a pile of papers fell out. Spilling over the mat.

Robin shook his head, looked down at his trembling hand and at the wine which was pouring across the small table, lapping its edge, slopping onto his trousers and shoes.

'Damn!' he said, 'Damn it. Bloody damn it!'

Free Hugs

We walked along by Central Park until we came to the right spot, but still we couldn't be sure.

'It doesn't look much,' Cindy said. 'I thought it would be bigger.'

I asked a man who was passing, 'Excuse me, is that the Dakota Building?'

'Yeah, that's it. But you couldn't afford to live there.' He looked at my Patti Smith tee-shirt. 'And neither could she.'

Cindy looked up and down the street, and through the railings of the park. 'So what'll we do now?'

'Let's go to Chinatown and buy a ten-dollar watch.'

'Why do you want to do that?'

'So when we go home and people look at my big gold Rolex, I can say – It's a ten-dollar watch – I got it in New York! Anyway we haven't got much money left to do anything else.'

*

We took the subway downtown. After I bought the biggest watch I could find and strapped it on my wrist, we walked along Canal Street. Near the corner of Broadway a group of people gathered around a man who was sitting at a small table. He pushed three cups around on the table top, rolling a silver ball between them and muttering, 'Just put your money down and tell me where it is. Just put your money down.'

A young guy in a cheap brown suit stepped up and put five dollars on the table. The man covered the ball and moved the little cups around slowly with the tips of his fingers. He stopped and the young guy tapped a cup. The man lifted it and there was nothing underneath. He scratched his head, bit his lip, put ten more dollars down. The cups moved. He tapped, he lost again. Then a third time.

'Cindy,' I said. 'It's easy. What's he doing? I can see where it is. It's easy.'

He turned away and the man started again, 'Just put your money down.'

I took ten dollars out of my pocket and put it on the table. He covered the ball and moved the cups backwards and forwards, looping them around, weaving a lazy pattern. I watched my cup. I never took my eyes off it. When he stopped, I tapped the one with the ball. He lifted it and it was empty. Then he lifted one of the other cups and there it was.

I stepped back, blinking. 'What happened? What?'

'You bet, mister, and you lost.'

The guy in the brown suit stood next to him grinning.

Cindy looked at me, then walked away. I skittled after her. 'Where are you going?' I said.

'Remember that girl near the park, the one with the cardboard sign?'

'Yeah?'

'You remember what it said?'

'Yeah. It said free hugs.'

'I'm going back to see if she's still there. I'm going to get a free hug. What are you going to do?'

Intensive Care

The last thing I remember before the nurses held me down was kicking at an IV stand and shouting, 'Get that fucking thing away from me!' Then I pulled at the ventilation hood and tried to prise it off my head, begging them to give me a catheter. I don't know why pissing seemed more important than breathing then. Priorities must get confused when your brain's deprived of oxygen.

When I woke again I was in a dark room. Electrodes were attached to my chest, and to my wrists and ankles. A tube taped to the side of my face was stuck into my right nostril. Another heavier tube pulled down on the corner of my mouth, making me drool. I was told later that this one went straight into my lungs and was breathing for me. Keeping me alive.

I could see someone in the corner of the room sitting in dim lamplight reading a thick file of papers. When I tried to speak, he came over and put a pad and pencil in my hand.

I wrote, 'How long?'

'Forty-eight hours,' he said. 'You were brought here from Ward 33 two days ago.'

Other nurses came and went. They checked my blood oxygen levels and ECG readings, changed the IV drips and emptied the urine bag. They'd obviously given me the catheter I had shouted for. The nurse in the corner was there all the time, sitting, watching and reading.

I asked for my phone, propped it on my chest and pressed *Music*. The first title on the screen was *Blood on the Tracks* and I listened to it on repeat for the rest of the day and through the night until the battery ran out.

And as the songs played, thin and brittle from the phone's tiny speaker, the hallucinations started. I stared up at the ceiling, watching storms blowing across open plains. I saw white barns and horses, barbed wire and mud. People wrapped in blankets walked down an empty street towards fishing boats in a fog-filled harbour. I sat in a bar room with old portraits on the walls, and playing cards flew and twisted through the smoky air. Every scene was monochrome, rough-edged and slow-moving, as they passed in front of my open eyes.

Next day the breathing tube was removed and I could sit up in bed. The nurse in the corner left his desk and came back with a bowl of water and a towel. He started sponging my arms and legs.

'We were worried about you,' he said. 'We weren't sure you'd make it.'

'You must have saved my life.'

'I think Bob Dylan did that. Well, maybe him and the drugs.'

Pontburn Wood

For the first seven days they scoured his bones. Chemicals dripped through a tube in the wall of his chest, seeping into a vein near the heart.

> *I walked into the wood, opened the gate and crossed the*
> *stream. Snow hard under my feet, icicles dropping*
> *below the bridge. The water slipped away in the dark.*

Then his skin reddened in welts and pustules across his stomach and his legs. He held ice in his mouth to cool the corrosive burn. The doctor lifted the sheet, sighed and said, 'Bless you.'

> *The trees in the wood were swaying, breaking light*
> *from the sky. The clouds shot through with acid colours.*
> *I staggered forward, cradling my arms.*

In the second week he bloated. A stone's weight of water in his feet and knees. He spent days and nights pissing into bottles, thinking of his mother crying for the pain in her swollen legs.

The snow melted and the river filled, edging its banks and flowing into new paths. I stepped over fallen branches sliding through the marginal scum.

On the twentieth day his scalp loosened. He stood in front of the mirror and pulled his hair, piece by piece, into the sink. The nurse brought a razor to complete the work.

The sun broke through, and the wet earth shone. I saw snowdrops and aconites as I passed. The wood stood naked, poised.

After a month he left the isolation room, too weak and tired to stand, shoes flapping. A stranger came and tied his laces, then smiled and walked away.

It took four weeks of dreaming to walk the miles through Pontburn Wood, tracing the path of new blood and bone.

The stories

Many of the stories in this collection were first read and critiqued by members of writing classes organised by thi wurd in 2021 and 2022, so thanks are due to Alan McMunnigall and all the writers in the group for their support and encouragement.

The Gift was first published online by *Product Magazine* in March 2022.

The Japanese Library was published by thi wurd in the anthology *Alternating Current* in November 2022.

The Longhouse was published in *Travels and Tribulations*, an anthology from Acid Bath Publishing in February 2022.

Aniela and James: a love story was shortlisted for the Short Fiction/University of Essex International Short Story Prize 2022.

The Life and Sulphurous Death of Theo D was longlisted for the Short Fiction/University of Essex International Short Story Prize 2021, and for the Galley Beggar Press Short Story Prize 2021/22. It was published online by Galley Beggar Press in March 2022.

Several of the stories in Intensive Care were published as a limited edition chapbook by Hickathrift Press in June 2022.

A Hat was longlisted for the Reflex Fiction Flash Fiction Prize Autumn 2022.

Wednesday Morning will be included in a new anthology on addiction and recovery from Acid Bath Publishing in 2023.

Pontburn Wood first appeared with the alternative title Blood Cancer in *The Middle of a Sentence*, a short prose anthology published by The Common Breath in December 2020.